EVERYONE LOVES

MR. AND MRS. BUNNY—
DETECTIVES EXTRAORDINAIRE!

An Amazon Best Book of the Year

A *Washington Post* Best Children's Book of the Year

"Has both the look and feel of a classic children's book."
—*The Washington Post*

"[Horvath's] fuzzy detectives will give younger readers
something they can readily grasp and enjoy."
—*The New York Times*

★ "An instant classic . . . begging to be read aloud."
—*Booklist,* Starred

★ "Look not for logic; this is a romp."
—*The Horn Book Magazine,* Starred

★ "Energetic pacing, witty prose, and snappy
dialogue coalesce in what is hopefully the first of many
escapades for these unforgettable, bumbling
would-be sleuths."
—*Publishers Weekly,* Starred

MORE PRAISE FOR

MR. AND MRS. BUNNY—
DETECTIVES EXTRAORDINAIRE!

"Mysteries within mysteries, witty (and witless) detectives, bunnies in fedoras and disco boots. It doesn't get any better— or funnier—than this! The off-the-wall humor and ridiculous plot twists will have you laughing out loud and begging for more."   —James Howe, author of the Bunnicula series

"Young readers will laugh out loud at the hapless Mr. and Mrs. Bunny, who manage to solve mysteries with plenty of enthusiasm but surprisingly little insight. (They firmly believe that their fedoras make them detectives.) A visit to the world of bunnies is memorable, from the revelation that a marmot, when wrung out properly, can make a squeegee, to the notion that rabbits can drive humans' cars as long as they wear platform shoes to act as pedal-extenders. Bravo, Mr. and Mrs. Bunny!" —Ann Martin, author of the Baby-Sitters Club series

MR. AND MRS. BUNNY—
DETECTIVES EXTRAORDINAIRE!

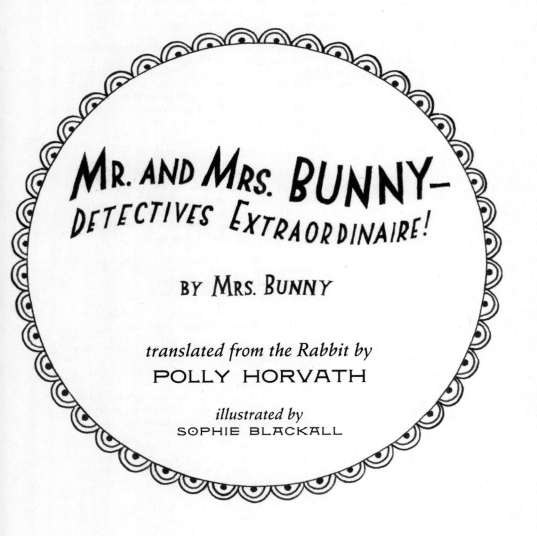

Mr. and Mrs. Bunny—
Detectives Extraordinaire!

by Mrs. Bunny

translated from the Rabbit by
POLLY HORVATH

illustrated by
SOPHIE BLACKALL

A YEARLING BOOK

Text copyright © 2012 by Polly Horvath
Illustrations copyright © 2012 by Sophie Blackall

All rights reserved. Published in the United States by Yearling, an imprint of Random House Children's Books, a division of Random House LLC, a Penguin Random House Company, New York. Originally published in hardcover in the United States by Schwartz & Wade Books, an imprint of Random House Children's Books, a division of Random House LLC, New York, in 2012.

Yearling and the jumping horse design are registered trademarks of Random House LLC.

Visit us on the Web! randomhouse.com/kids

Educators and librarians, for a variety of teaching tools, visit us at RHTeachersLibrarians.com

The Library of Congress has cataloged the hardcover edition of this work as follows:
Horvath, Polly.
Mr. and Mrs. Bunny—detectives extraordinaire! / Polly Horvath. —1st ed.
p. cm.
Summary: Middle-schooler Madeline's hippy parents have been kidnapped from Hornby Island, Canada, by foxes and Madeline, upon discovering that she can understand animal languages, hires two rabbit detectives to find them.
ISBN 978-0-375-86755-2 (trade) — ISBN 978-0-375-96755-9 (glb) — ISBN 978-0-375-89827-3 (ebook)
[1. Human-animal communication—Fiction. 2. Kidnapping—Fiction. 3. Rabbits—Fiction. 4. Foxes—Fiction. 5. Marmots—Fiction. 6. Hippies—Fiction. 7. Hornby Island (B.C. : Island)—Fiction. 8. Mystery and detective stories.] I. Title.
PZ7.H79224Mr 2011
[Fic]—dc22
2010024133

ISBN 978-0-375-86530-5 (pbk.)

Printed in the United States of America

10 9 8 7 6 5 4 3

First Yearling Edition 2014

To Mr. Bunny, of course!

And to rabbits everywhere.

❀❦ CONTENTS ❦❀

⊰SUMMER SOLSTICE⊱

*B*y nighttime Hornby Island would be a blaze of lights. It was the summer solstice, and for the festival of Luminara all the scattered squatters and homeowners were making luminaries to celebrate the day of longest light.

Madeline, walking home from the ferries her last day of school, wondered why they celebrated a long day of light with more light. They celebrate the shortest days with lights, winter solstice with lights and the long days of summer with lights. Lights, lights, lights. What's wrong with a little dark? If we didn't spend so much on candles, maybe we'd have money for shoes.

Hornby was a very small island east of Vancouver Island. Madeline lived there with her parents, Flo and Mildred, for so they asked to be called by everyone, including Madeline, even though their names were Harry and Denise. Flo and Mildred were hippies who had started out in San Francisco but migrated north. There they joined the rest of the family, who were living not one hundred percent legally in Canada, spread out on Vancouver Island and the Gulf Islands. When Flo and Mildred got to Hornby Island, they came into their own by discovering that with very little effort they could both play the marimba and make jewelry out of sand dollars. There was no stopping them after that.

As nature often has it, they had a child who did not want to join them in their all-day pursuit of enlightenment and a better mung bean. Instead, she became very good at cooking and cleaning and sewing and bookkeeping and minor household repairs. She was the one who changed the lightbulbs. When only ten, she got herself a waitress job part-time at the Happy Goat Café, a fine establishment of three tables, some tree stumps, the owner (KatyD) and a resident goat. Madeline managed to earn enough money there that if the sand-dollar art had a slow month or two, they still managed to get by.

All the other children on Hornby were homeschooled, but Madeline preferred to get up at five every morning and walk to the harbor, where she took a ferry to Denman Island, the bus across Denman, the ferry to Vancouver Island and then the bus that took her to a real school. She had made the decision to do this when she entered grade five and was finally old enough to make the trip without help. This earned her the reputation for being eccentric, but the happy hippies of Hornby were tolerant of Madeline, if a little wary. Mostly they felt sorry for Flo and Mildred, raising an oddball like that.

The children in Madeline's school were less tolerant. The students who came from other tiny islands like Hornby usually wore homemade natural fabrics and, often, tie-dyed clothes. They bathed infrequently because water on the small islands was scarce. They never had money for field trips, and a good portion of them didn't seem to brush their hair. Madeline was as neat and clean as she could be, but her clothes were never in style or even always in one piece, and she was the only child who had ever come all the way from Hornby. This alone made her suspect.

Madeline's schoolmates, raised in more mainstream, connected-to-the-rest-of-the-world ways, thought all children from the smaller islands were holier-than-thou, attached to bizarre goddess-worshipping religions, and surly. Madeline didn't start out surly, but she quickly *became* surly. She didn't know how to make the other children like her, and she felt she constantly had to defend herself from unspoken accusations about a way of life she hadn't chosen to begin with. Well, she thought, who needs them? I bet none of them know how to make plumbing repairs. I bet none of them have read *Pride and Prejudice*. Twice.

On this summer solstice day, the last day of school, she *really* felt surly. Her teacher had announced that Prince Charles, who was doing a Canadian tour, was stopping on Vancouver Island and visiting one school! And that school was theirs! He was going to grace them with his presence at the graduation ceremony for grades four, five and six. He was *personally* going to give out the awards! The children who had won awards would get them from Prince Charles himself! Because of this, today they would be making special white tissue paper graduation gowns, which they would decorate with red maple leaves, and for graduation were requested to wear white shoes to match. If they did not own white shoes, they could be purchased cheaply at Walmart—no one need go out of their way to get expensive white shoes, Madeline's teacher stressed. She was sure all parents would be amenable to this. After all, it wasn't every day that *Prince Charles* made an appearance at your graduation ceremony! Such an honor would probably never come again!

Madeline's heart sank. Mildred got Madeline's shoes from the Salvation Army. They were usually serviceable, scuffed and ugly. Often they were the wrong size, because there was never much choice. Madeline knew that even if she could convince her mother to take her to the Salvation Army store, the chance of just happening to find white shoes was unlikely. Graduation was in a week. What waitressing money Madeline had, Mildred had already spent on Luminara.

Of course Madeline knew she didn't *have* to go to graduation. But she had won the reading award and the music award and the writing award. Three awards her first year in a real school! She wanted to stand on the stage and collect them. She wanted Prince Charles to hand them to her in front of all the kids who didn't talk to her because she was "islandy" and "homeschooly."

"Come look at this luminary," called Flo from the porch as Madeline made her way up their driftwood-lined walkway.

"I've been working on it all day. See, it's got this lacework picture of sheep."

"Nice," said Madeline, and sat with a thump.

"So—school's out. Hallelujah," said Flo. He waited for Madeline to say something else about his luminaries. Usually she was supportive of his artwork. When she didn't praise them further, he eyed her warily.

"Of course, there's still the graduation ceremony," said Madeline. She paused. "Did you hear Prince Charles was coming to Vancouver Island?"

Flo laughed. "Yeah? You planning to lead the ticker-tape parade?"

"No," said Madeline. "But he's coming to our school. He's coming to our graduation ceremony!"

"Oh, for heaven's sakes," said Flo. "That. You don't really want to go to *that,* do you? You know I never even went to my college grad. Pointless thing. What does it mean, really? And the monarchy! Please! What a bunch of crap. Queen of Canada. Come on, Madeline. You can't say it's anything but a bunch of nonsense. Look at all her money. Richest woman in the world. They ought to split her money up among the poor in England. Do you know what their unemployment rate is

like? Instead, they send this silly man around Canada to attend children's silly graduation ceremonies. Get real."

"I couldn't go if I wanted to. I need white shoes," said
Madeline.

"They can't make you wear white shoes!" said Flo. "Wear
the shoes you have. That'll show them."

"No, my teacher said we have to wear white shoes to go
with our white tissue paper gowns. We *have* to."

"Nonsense. Sending people out to buy white shoes when
they have perfectly good brown ones! Bunch of crap. You see
how our consumer culture has infiltrated everything? God, I
wouldn't go to some ceremony given by people whose *raison
d'être* is to pressure children into buying shoes they *don't need*
to stand in front of some pointless outdated symbol of colo-
nialism."

Flo started to go back into the house, shaking his head.

"I DO need them," muttered Madeline, watching his re-
treating back.

"You *do* need them?" said Flo, turning back to face her.

"Prince Charles is giving out the awards himself. I won
three," said Madeline. "I can't go up there in brown shoes."

"I'll tell you what, Madeline," said Flo. "If you can tell me

what makes him so special that you have to put on white shoes for him; if you can *explain* it in a way that makes sense, then I will attend the ceremony. But I would bet you a pair of white shoes that you cannot. This goes against everything we have tried to teach you."

Madeline frowned. Flo nodded, triumphant at her silence, and went inside.

Madeline went down to the garden, where her mother was stringing luminaries between the beans.

"Hi," said Madeline.

"Happy Luminara!"

"Prince Charles is coming to our school."

"Oh, for heaven's sake. Better not tell Flo. Aren't these luminaries pretty? Oh, and Danika has made some giant animal-shaped ones. Giant deer and strange Martianlike figures and *salamanders*. I just love salamanders, don't you? They always look so magical."

"Yeah, they're okay," said Madeline, eating a bean. "Next week at graduation, he's coming. It's kind of once-in-a-lifetime."

"Speaking of once-in-a-lifetime, Danika says the paper is so thin you can only use them once. She says they're thaumaturgic when lit. She's going to bring them early because they take a while to set up. We're going to scatter them through the woods for people to happen on when we do our midnight lantern walk."

"How many candles do they take?"

"Lots. I think they're the biggest luminaries anyone's made yet. One of them is ten feet."

"All those candles drip drip drip, gone by morning. I don't suppose there's any waitressing money left?" asked Madeline.

"Not a penny. I had to buy more art supplies. Flo needed paper to make some new luminaries and we had to fix some of the ones that got torn last year."

"And tomorrow all those luminaries will be done with. Dollars' and dollars' worth."

"We can recycle most of them for next year."

"But not the candles. We'll have just burnt up all that money. I thought we were supposed to be conserving resources and living green. How green is it to use a bunch of candles on one night of fun?"

"That's true, but think, Madeline, it's like the Zen sand mandalas. Remember when the monks came and spent all day meticulously making a detailed picture on the beach with colored sand and then at the end of the day this great and detailed creation was borne away by the tides? Nothing lasts. Besides, Luminara is part of our great cultural heritage."

"Luminara was invented by Zanky Marsala one night when she was in a hyperspiritual state."

"Hyperspiritual state? What do we, uh, mean by that?" asked Mildred, looking a little nervous.

"KatyD told me that. So clearly it's just a made-up holiday."

"Luminara is a lovely tradition. And all holidays are made up. And lots of things of enduring mysticism come from people being in, well, more-than-average spiritual states. Look at Stonehenge."

"I need shoes."

"No, you don't," said Mildred, surprised at the sudden change of subject and looking down at Madeline's feet. "You only have one tiny hole in that one." She pointed.

"I need white shoes for graduation."

"Oh, those things they dream up at the end of the year. God, that's why I didn't want you to go to school. All this business of grading and this person is better than that person. And we all have to dress alike. It's so meaningless, Madeline. And graduation is just a silly artificial rite."

"Well, you could say that about anything. You could say that about Luminara."

Mildred sighed again, stopped threading the luminaries among the bean strings, and leaned down to look Madeline in the eye.

"Luminara celebrates light and our connection to Mother Earth. What is a graduation? It's just another way of brainwashing you into believing that achievement is the answer. Of course you must make your own choices, but I wouldn't go if I were you."

Then she straightened up and went back to stringing lights.

"Prince Charles thinks it's important enough to come!" said Madeline as a parting shot.

"Don't get me started on the monarchy!" warned Mildred as Madeline headed to the house. "Sometimes I wonder where you came from. You're not like anyone in the family except Uncle Runyon."

"I LIKE Uncle Runyon!" called Madeline over her shoulder.

"So do I," said her mother, shaking her head. "But I don't understand either of you."

Uncle Runyon was the only relative living on Vancouver Island one hundred percent legally and with consistently covered toes. He worked as a secret decoder scientist for the Canadian government. No one was supposed to know where he lived because it was top-secret, but he had the family over for Easter every year anyway and he attended what celebrations of theirs he could stand. He always said all this hush-hush business concerning him was just a lot of hooey. No enemy spies were interested in *him*. His job was really very boring.

Or so he had always told Madeline. But out there on Vancouver Island somewhere there was suddenly a group becoming very, very interested in him indeed.

➤THE SURPRISE◄

Mr. and Mrs. Bunny had a problem. The winter on Mount Washington had been hard. Mr. Bunny had had to shovel snow from the doorway of their hutch nearly every day. On top of that, their whole litter of twelve rabbits had grown up and moved far away. The closest one was in Australia. Not only was the hutch too big, but its large empty rooms depressed Mrs. Bunny. And there weren't any other bunny neighbors, particularly female ones, for Mrs. Bunny to cavort with and form clubs with. But it was the snow that they had found so unsettling. It had damaged their roof and left them stranded for two weeks in January. Although it had long ago melted,

Mrs. Bunny still spent a lot of time remembering it. Remembering snow was not how she liked to occupy her bunny brain.

"After all," said Mrs. Bunny, "we are not arctic hares! We do not snow-proof our hutches. We do not keep snowshoes in our cupboards!"

"Yes," said Mr. Bunny. "It has occurred to me, *more than once*, Mrs. Bunny, that perhaps it was time to move!"

"Oh, Mr. Bunny, my idea exactly!" said Mrs. Bunny.

"All right then. Let's find a smaller hutch."

"In a valley," said Mrs. Bunny.

"In a valley."

"With lots of vegetables."

"Or vegetable-growing potential."

It was Mr. Bunny's harebrained idea, which surfaced now and again, that he and Mrs. Bunny should grow all their own food. Mrs. Bunny, who had seen Mr. Bunny's experiments with roses, dahlias and the ever-hardy lavender plant, had great misgivings.

"A good growing climate," said Mrs. Bunny tactfully.

"And no marmots," said Mr. Bunny.

"Definitely no marmots," said Mrs. Bunny.

Marmots, of course, were the bane of many a bunny's

existence. With their constant whining and tendency to matted fur, no one wanted to live around a marmot. Except perhaps another marmot. And sometimes not even they.

"Well, then, I think we have a reasonable list of wants and needs. I shall roller-skate down the mountain and find a bunny realtor and see what's what." Mr. Bunny often invented things and just that morning had invented some roller skates for hopping. He had not yet had a chance to try them out.

"Yes, you do that," said Mrs. Bunny, who wanted to get back to her fitness routine. She didn't like Mr. Bunny around for this. He tended to make remarks.

Mr. Bunny put on his rollerhoppers, as he called them, and hopskated right down the mountain. You can imagine how difficult that must be, rollerhopping, but Mr. Bunny was grace personified. He didn't return until dinner.

"Well, Mrs. Bunny," he said, coming in all pink-cheeked and proud of himself. "I have a great surprise for you."

"You have found a realtor," said Mrs. Bunny, dishing him up a nice steaming bowl of carrot stew, then joining him at the table.

"Better! I have bought us a new hutch!" said Mr. Bunny. "The deed is done! We can move in next week!"

There was a stunned silence.

"Well?" said Mr. Bunny finally. "I thought you'd be hopping around with happiness."

Mrs. Bunny, who had gotten up to get Mr. Bunny some bread, sat down again with a thump.

"No bread?" asked Mr. Bunny, who sometimes wasn't very good at telling from which direction the wind blew.

Mrs. Bunny put her head down on the table.

"Uh-oh," said Mr. Bunny.

They sat in silence for a long time, listening to the ticking of the clock. Finally Mr. Bunny lifted Mrs. Bunny's ears so he could see her face and try to tell exactly what kind of mood she had fallen prey to.

"Mrs. Bunny?" he whispered. "Hello, hello, anyone in there?"

"Mr. Bunny," said Mrs. Bunny finally.

"Yes? For so I am called," said Mr. Bunny.

"Hutch buying is something rabbits do *IN PAIRS*."

"Mrs. Bunny, I am sure you are only hungry. Once you have a little carrot stew in you, this mood of yours will pass in a trice."

"DON'T TELL ME ABOUT MY MOODS!" began Mrs.

Bunny, and that is when Mr. Bunny, in one of his few smart moves that day, pulled out the picture of the hutch and shoved it in her face.

"SEE?" said Mr. Bunny, a trifle hysterically. "SEE?"

Mrs. Bunny did see—a sweet little thatched white cottage with light blue shutters and a light blue door. There was a lovely wreath around the door knocker and roses twining about the gate.

"You see," said Mr. Bunny. "It is as sweet and adorable as Mrs. Bunny herself."

"How many bedrooms?"

"Three. One for us and two for any Bunnys who come back to visit. It is unlikely we will ever see all twelve at the same time."

Mrs. Bunny began to look sad, so Mr. Bunny distracted her by telling her again that the hutch was as sweet as she was. "Also, therealeastateagentsaiditwillprobablytakea-verylongtimetosellourhousebecausebunniesaren'tbuyingin-themountainsanymore. You ARE so sweet, Mrs. Bunny. You should have a hutch as sweet as you." Yeah, he said to himself craftily, bury the lead.

"Nothing could be *that* sweet," said Mrs. Bunny. Then she

studied the picture more closely. "But it *is* nice. Of course, the former owners will take that wreath with them. That will detract from its sweetness a bit."

"Oh no, that's the kicker," said Mr. Bunny. "They're leaving such things behind."

"Well . . . ," said Mrs. Bunny, unwilling to let Mr. Bunny off a hook she had him so securely hung from, "I admit that from outside appearances it seems . . . nice."

"Nice, Mrs. Bunny? Nice? How many times has Mr. Bunny heard you say that if you ever found a house with both birdbaths and garden gnomes you would move right in?"

"Is it marmot-free?"

"Well, no place is marmot-*free*, Mrs. Bunny. Let us not dwell in fools' paradises."

"We shall have to buy furniture!" said Mrs. Bunny, determined to find a fly in the ointment, and now she had, because Mr. Bunny, in his honeymoon period with Krazy Glue, had glued all their furniture to the floor. "That will cost money." Mr. Bunny did so hate to spend money.

"*Au contraire!* I was saving the best for last! The former owners disappeared rather suddenly, so the house is to be sold *fully furnished*. And I have it on the best authority that the house is brimming, absolutely brimming, Mrs. Bunny, with country-cottage-style antiques. When I asked the realtor if they could be decoupaged he said they were fairly begging for it."

"He would. Besides, Mr. Bunny, the decoupage phase is over, in case you had not noticed. That train has left the station," said Mrs. Bunny crushingly.

"Or just as lovely not decoupaged," said Mr. Bunny hastily. He never could keep track of Mrs. Bunny's hobbies. She was a bunny of sudden short-lived enthusiasms. "I myself enjoy an unpainted piece of furniture, so this fails to disappoint *me*. Well, Mrs. Bunny, have I not found the perfect hutch despite your crankiness and many unreasonable demands?"

"Hmm." Then something new struck her. It struck her like a gong. Her long and fuzzy ears quivered. "Mr. Bunny, you say that these bunnies *disappeared*?"

"Did I say that?" asked Mr. Bunny, looking suddenly nervous.

"Your very words."

"Well, uh—"

"And *where* did you say this hutch was? This hutch so suddenly vacated by the previous bunnies? Vacated so hastily that all the furniture and whatnots were included."

"Uh—"

"Where, Mr. Bunny? Out with it."

"Rabbitville, down in the Cowichan Valley. A charming valley of mild and temperate climate."

"And *foxes*!"

"Oh, Mrs. Bunny, rumors, idle chitchat, tittle-tattle."

"I would lay odds, Mr. Bunny, that foxes is what happened to these former owners."

"I'm sure if that were the case the realtor would have mentioned it."

"I'm sure he would not. Tell me, Mr. Bunny, did they also leave all their clothes, these previous owners?"

"Yes, and a fine automobile," said Mr. Bunny.

"Foxes. You may be sure of it," said Mrs. Bunny. "Bunnies do not leave their clothes to be sold as part of the house unless they have met with a bad end."

"Oh well, look at lightning," said Mr. Bunny. "Never strikes in the same place twice."

"Lightning does not strike twice, Mr. Bunny; foxes, on the

other hand, probably regard the houses in Rabbitville as a strip of fast-food joints. I, personally, don't want to be someone's Big Mac."

"Nonsense. Don't you think we'd have heard if there was a large fox problem? It certainly would be in the *Bunny Gazette.*"

"Oh well, I suppose done is done," said Mrs. Bunny, cheerfully digging into her carrot stew.

"Oh, and Mrs. Bunny?" said Mr. Bunny, after he had finished his stew in welcome silence. "I forgot to tell you the best part."

"There's more?" said Mrs. Bunny, not without sarcasm.

"Yes, a great deal more. You know how you have always wanted to hop around a manor hutch?"

"Yes?" said Mrs. Bunny.

"Like in those Bunny Austen books you read where rabbits live in great parks with manor hutches?"

"Yes?"

"Well, there's a manor house right up the road."

"A hutch or a house?" asked Mrs. Bunny.

"Well, it is a house. It is a human habitat. But still . . ."

"Yes, still . . . ," said Mrs. Bunny, dropping her spoon in delight and forgetting to look disapproving. There was never much chance of getting invited into a human house. You either ended up as dinner or a pet. But she did so want to see the inside of one of these places.

Mr. Bunny smiled. He had her now. "Yes. By my fuzzy ears and whiskers, a manor house for Mrs. Bunny to obsess over. And to think, we'll be able to see it from our own garden! We have a splendid view of the whole valley. I can putter around with my saws and hammers. You can join some clubs. And we can settle back and wait for the baby Bunnys to come visit with their own baby bunnies someday, perhaps."

"Oh," said Mrs. Bunny in a frenzy of ecstasy. "Mr. Bunny, you *have* done well!"

"Yes, I have, Mrs. Bunny, and now we can spend the rest of our days leading a peaceful quiet life."

But that was where Mr. Bunny was wrong.

⊁LUMINARA⊁

Madeline and Mildred and Flo gathered on the front porch as the neighbors started arriving.

It was the tradition on Luminara for everyone to trip from house to house viewing everyone else's luminaries. The children paraded their paper lanterns from one end of the island to the next. After they were put to bed, the adults had their own lantern walk.

Madeline had always loved Luminara; even now, upset as she was to have had all her shoe money spent on candles, she couldn't help feeling a thrill to see her neighbors dressed in the traditional Luminara costumes, long white gauzy dresses for the women, velvet breeches or white robes (their pick) for the men. The children, dressed as fairies and butterflies and gauzy birds, becoming for a few hours the small winged creatures of the night.

Mildred offered everyone cheese straws made with locally sourced organic raw milk cheese while Flo kept asking who was available for the marimba band. Everyone on Hornby played the marimba, and several played ukuleles.

"Want to play in the marimba band tonight, Madeline? Oh, and Zanky said that KatyD asked if you'd help out tonight at the Happy Goat? Sunshine can't come in, she's sick. I said that you probably didn't want to miss Luminara. And you'd probably rather make music than money."

Shoe money! Madeline thought.

"You'll miss the lantern walk with the other children," said Mildred.

"Why don't I stay up for the adult one and go with you? You know, Flo, you almost got lost in the dark last year and I had to come out with a flashlight and find you."

"Oh yeah," said Flo. "Well, sure, Mildred and I always say you're the adult in the family."

Madeline went inside and changed into her gauzy white

Luminara dress and then skedaddled to the café. When she got there KatyD said, "Thank goodness. I've been trying to cook and waitress. All the tables and both stumps are filled and people keep coming."

"Where is our hummus?" an angry woman screamed just before the goat walked over and peed on her.

"*What* did your goat just do?" spluttered the woman, standing up in disbelief.

She must be visiting the island, thought Madeline. Anyone who came to the Happy Goat regularly knew that the goat was always peeing on people. No one ever got used to it, exactly, but no one ever did anything about it either.

"Madeline, grab her some paper napkins, and then start taking orders," called KatyD, who was trying to wash dishes and crumble tofu all at once.

Madeline gave the woman a handful of napkins and a sympathetic look, but the woman just dried herself off and stomped angrily away. Madeline didn't have time to worry about it. People coming in from other islands to see the luminaries were lining up for a table or stump. Before long she was serving them on the ground as families grabbed menus and sat down wherever there was space and the goat hadn't peed.

At ten o'clock KatyD closed the café and handed Madeline a fistful of dollars. "Want me to walk you home?"

"That's okay, the road is lit with luminaries," said Madeline. She could hardly wait to get alone and count her money. She was sure she had enough for shoes.

It was gloaming when she left the café, but by the time she came to the path in the woods it was full dark. The giant moon glimmered as if it were a luminary itself, awash in orange candlelight. Stars twinkled. The woods, lit from within, glowed with a faint green phosphorus light. She bet if you could look at the earth from space, it would be glittering too, a giant planetary luminary.

She sat right down for a second in the middle of the woods to enjoy it all.

Meanwhile, unbeknownst to Madeline, back at her house, sinister forces were at work. A car had just pulled into the driveway and four foxes dressed in trench coats, scarves and sunglasses had gotten out. The fox in the center, the Grand Poobah, as he was known, carried a small file card box. The other foxes surrounded him as he walked straight up to Flo and Mildred, who were busy reassembling a giant luminary that had toppled over.

"Hail, humans!" said the Grand Poobah. Actually what he said was "Hail, hoomans!" He had just learned English, and he insisted that all the foxes do likewise, as humans would inevitably be too stupid to understand Fox. But his reading vocabulary was larger than his speaking vocabulary, so that he made the occasional pronunciation mistake.

"Oh, look," said Mildred, grabbing Flo's arm. "One of the families has dressed up in fox costumes. Isn't that adorable?"

"Cool, man," said Flo, going up to greet them and pulling gently at one of the foxes' fur. "Where'd you get the duds, man?"

"OUCH!" screamed the fox. "Poobah, make him stop."

"Now, now, be nice. We come in peace. Ahem! Ladies and gentlemen," began the Grand Poobah, for this was how he had heard humans address each other on TV. "Ladies and gentlemen, we are in need of assistance. You see, we are opening a factory soon. Fanny Fox's Canned Rabbit Products and By-products. Fanny Fox, perhaps the greatest chef of all time, finally gave consent for us to mass-produce all her rabbit recipes. We have here her full collection on handy-dandy file cards." He pointed to the box he was carrying. "Unfortunately, last night Fanny died."

"Tough break, dude, but at least you've got the recipes," said Flo. He turned to Mildred. "Man, *what* was in those cheese straws? These can't be people dressed in fox costumes. Unless they're, like, little people."

"Tough break indeed," said the Grand Poobah, ignoring Flo's last comment. "Fanny loved the idea of becoming famous. She was so proud of having the factory named after her that she had recipe cards and stationery engraved with the factory name and logo at the top. And because she planned to sell to you hoomans, she had the factory name done in English as well as Fox. Very considerate, we foxes are."

"Maybe," said Flo. "But what the heck is a hooman?"

"She had the logo tattooed on her paws," piped up one of the bodyguards. "She was, like, nuts when it came to that logo."

"Speak when you are spoken to, Filbert," said the Grand Poobah. "And try not to adopt the hooman's verbal tics. Flo, a hooman is you, man, mwa-haha!"

"I didn't know that foxes were, like, so commercial," said Flo.

"Foxes are titans of industry. Have you never heard of Fox

Studios? Fox Television? You didn't think it was owned by hoomans, did you? I myself could have been a movie star. As you see, I have the exceedingly good looks and overweening ego, but, alas, someone had to stay and take care of the den."

The Grand Poobah stopped and batted his long eyelashes. Then he realized they couldn't be seen behind his sunglasses, so he took them off and batted his eyelashes again, first at Flo and then at Mildred. They continued to stare blankly.

"But back to matters at hand," the Grand Poobah said, clearing his throat and putting his sunglasses back on. "We have the recipes, true, but we can't *read* the recipes. Fanny was always terrified that someone from a rival firm would steal them, so she wrote them all in code."

He opened the box and took out one of the file cards to show Flo and Mildred. On the top was engraved FANNY FOX'S CANNED RABBIT PRODUCTS AND BY-PRODUCTS FACTORY. There was a logo of a fox trying to cram a protesting rabbit into a pressure cooker.

Mildred flinched. "I'm a vegan myself," she said.

"Of course you are," said the Grand Poobah. "And your IQ is well under one hundred. Don't worry, we know all about hoomans. We've been studying your sitcoms. And we know all about the vegans. Interesting choice. Vegetables and grasses. Foxes, of course, prefer *meat*."

He smiled at them. It was a cruel smile that made the most of his prominent canines. The thought of meat had caused a little line of drool to escape his mouth and make its way down his chin. Mildred flinched again.

"Did someone say something about, uh, grasses?" asked Flo, whose attention had flagged. "I'm not a vegan. Anyone want a cheese straw? The milk is locally sourced."

Mildred studied the card some more. Underneath the factory name and logo were a series of wiggles and swirls. She passed the card to Flo.

"What's that, like, Fox alphabet?" asked Flo.

"Fox alphabet?" barked the Grand Poobah, and then recovered himself. "No, my dear sir, that is *code*. Unbreakable code, so it seems. That is why we have come to you. I have a cousin who lives in the woods by Ottawa who keeps track of government goings-on. It is, as I'm sure you can understand, important for our species to keep tabs on your species to see what little nasty thing you're going to be up to next. He found out some interesting items. One is that there are several decoder scientists sprinkled around Canada."

"Ha! Runyon said he was the only one! Ha!" said Flo.

"No, babe, he said he was the *best* one," said Mildred.

"Well, here is the salient point," interrupted the Grand Poobah, who was really losing patience with them and also thinking their fingers would make tasty snack food. "He is the *closest* one. To have a decoder actually on Vancouver Island is enormously convenient. Foxes hate to travel."

"The ferry was loathsome," said one of the bodyguard foxes. "I thought I was like to die."

"And we had to stay in the car the whole time with its blackened windows so as not to arouse suspicions," said another fox. "I got seasick."

"I had to use the bathroom," said another.

"I wanted a chocolate bar. They have vending machines on the ferry and I could have snuck inside without anyone seeing me. Foxes are very stealthy and humans never notice anything anyway. They're way too busy with their cell phones and iPods, but *he* wouldn't let us."

"Shut up, shut up, shut up, all of you," said the Grand Poobah. "Now, unfortunately, for all my Ottawa cousin's snooping, he couldn't obtain the decoder's *exact* address. That, apparently, is a secret. It is rumored this decoder is somewhere in the Cowichan Valley, where we are starting our factory. *Très coincidental, n'est-ce pas?* Our foxy Ottawa snoop *did* find out the address of the decoder's nearest relatives. That was no secret. And so, you see, here we are with you. And you, of course, will tell us where to find this relative of yours because we have been so friendly and haven't once munched on your digits, no matter how great the temptation." Another line of drool escaped the Poobah's lips and began its trail down his furry chin.

"Love to help you out, man, but I can't remember the address. Can you, Mildred?" asked Flo, scratching his chest.

"Well, now, let me think," said Mildred. "You know I'm not good with directions."

The Grand Poobah put the card back in the file and snapped it shut.

"So that's the way it's going to be, is it?"

"What way?" asked Mildred.

"Is there a way?" asked Flo, who was having a hard time keeping up.

Neither one of them had the slightest idea what the Grand Poobah was talking about. They didn't think it was a big deal to give Uncle Runyon's address to a bunch of foxes who needed recipes decoded. They were all for helping forest animals. They just couldn't remember where Uncle Runyon lived. Madeline always took care of details like that. And they were more than a little suspicious that they were hallucinating the whole thing anyway.

"Pretending you don't remember will get you nowhere. I'll give you one last chance to talk and then we will take you someplace where we can be, shall we say, more persuasive."

"Talk about what?" asked Flo.

"Do you really think I believe you can't remember where your own relative lives?" said the Poobah, leaning in menacingly, his meat-eating breath hot on Mildred's kneecap.

"But I really *don't* remember," said Mildred. Why didn't this fox believe her? People had accused her of many things before but never of insincerity. She found it very distressing. "Now, if you could wait until Madeline comes home . . ."

"Oh yes, the daughter. Give up your young like that, would you? I have a better idea—let's put a little leverage on the two of you *and* your daughter. Let's take you and leave her behind to stew. Let's see who cracks first."

"Cracks what, man?" asked Flo.

"We'll just write your little Madeline a note, shall we?" said the Grand Poobah.

"Felix, blow the whistle."

One of the trench-coated foxes took a large whistle out of his pocket and blew it. Immediately seventeen foxes popped out of the trunk of the car and surrounded Flo and Mildred. They were all flak-jacketed and carrying truncheons. Within seconds they had Flo and Mildred trussed up and gagged and placed in the trunk. Then the Grand Poobah whipped out a fountain pen and paper and wrote a note.

Dear Madeline,

We have taken your parents in for questioning. If they do not tell us where the decoder, aka Uncle Runyon, lives, foul things await them. Beware, if they do not talk, you will be next.

We will be in touch. Do not go to the police or we cannot answer for our actions. But let me give you one clue! Finger food! Mwa-haha.

Cordially yours,
The Enemy

The Grand Poobah tacked the note to the fridge, where he knew all humans left notes of importance.

One of his guard foxes rushed in.

"Hurry, boss, Fidel has finally managed to get the car started, but it's close quarters and the guys are beginning to nip at each other!"

Fidel, the driver, had to wear stilts to work the pedals. It sometimes took an hour for him to get the thing running.

"Can none of you behave with any dignity?" asked the Grand Poobah, and then, walking out in a stately, grand and poobahly manner, tripped over his tail and spilled recipe cards everywhere.

"Pick those up, will you?" he said to Felix, and proceeded into the car as if nothing had happened.

Felix scurried about, picking up the cards, then ran with them to the car, which was starting to pull away. Foxes were very bad about waiting for each other. He just had time to leap in before it headed off to the ferry.

The Grand Poobah took the cards with silent dignity and replaced them in the box.

"Change the radio channel, we shall listen to cool jazz," the Grand Poobah said.

"We want to hear easy listening!" whined the rest of the foxes.

It was just such things that made being Grand Poobah such a trial.

"Maybe we should ask the *hoomans* what they want to hear," he joked.

Everyone laughed uproariously, but they laughed at all his jokes or even when they thought he *might* be joking.

I *am* a funny guy, he thought. Then the car sped down the driveway, swerving suddenly to avoid a girl just coming out of the woods.

"Stupid hoomans, always underfoot," said the Grand Poobah as Fidel floored the gas pedal and the car sped on down the road.

"Hey!" shrieked Madeline, leaping out of the way. She had to sit down for a second to collect herself. This road was used so seldom, and certainly no one ever sped. She remained seated, panting for a moment. Who could that possibly have been? There appeared to be dozens of red eyes staring through blackened windows, and a fox driving. Before she could puzzle this out, a group of people in Luminara costumes arrived.

"Hi, Madeline," called another group who were standing on her front porch eating the cheese straws Mildred had left out. "Where's your folks?"

"I don't know," said Madeline. "Aren't they here?"

"I don't see them."

"Oh, they probably went over to Zanky's to help set up the marimbas."

"Well, happy Luminara."

Happy Luminara is right, thought Madeline, counting her money in the porch light. She had thirty-two dollars. She had shoes!

Madeline went inside to get a drink. Immediately she saw the note on the fridge and read it twice, frowning. Was this a joke? she wondered. No, it couldn't be a joke. It wasn't her parents' handwriting and no one else knew about Uncle Runyon. She sat down at the kitchen table to think.

She'd have to go to Uncle Runyon's.

Someone knocked on the door. She peeked out the window. It was the Zetmans from the harbor. She'd never be able to think if people kept coming every three seconds to see the luminaries. Madeline tiptoed into the bathroom and waited until they gave up and left, and then she went outside and blew out all the candles quickly, before anyone else could arrive. Now there was only moonlight. She looked at her watch. It was late to be making the journey, but she had no choice. There was one hour before the last ferry. She decided she'd better be on it.

Madeline changed into her blue jeans, put the note and her money in her back pocket and was starting down her driveway when she saw what looked like another note lying on the ground. She picked it up. It was a file card. At the top it said FANNY FOX'S CANNED RABBIT PRODUCTS AND BY-PRODUCTS FACTORY with a picture of a rabbit being shoved into a pressure cooker. It was such a dreadful picture that she flinched. Who would draw such a thing? Underneath were a series of squiggles and whirls. It was impossible to tell if it had anything to do with the note on the fridge, but it was an odd thing to find in her driveway so she put it in her sweater pocket just in case. Then she ran.

Madeline took the last ferry off the island, which connected her to the last bus on Denman and the final last ferry, to Vancouver Island. This got her into Comox in time to catch a bus to Duncan in the Cowichan Valley, where she got a cab. The cabdriver kept looking at her oddly. She guessed he wasn't used to driving little girls from bus stations in the middle of the night, but she had no time to worry about such things. He let her off at the bottom of Uncle Runyon's driveway. There goes my shoe money, she thought glumly as she paid him.

The driveway was lit by the remnants of a bonfire, its embers still smoking. Uncle Runyon's manservant, Jeeves, stood moodily in the background, watching the coals. It was his job to burn all the papers after they had been decoded. Uncle Runyon had told Madeline once that Jeeves loved bonfires. He would stand and watch until the last light left the last ember. Uncle Runyon was happy to provide him with this small pleasure. Jeeves knew nothing about what Uncle Runyon did for a living. He had no idea he was burning code. He thought Uncle Runyon was just another rich eccentric. Uncle Runyon encouraged this idea by giving Jeeves odd things to burn occasionally besides code: old shoes and throw pillows and bathroom mats. In fact, he kept the barn piled high with things to burn, including the daily files of decoded messages.

Madeline didn't stop to say hello; she had urgent business

and she didn't think Uncle Runyon would want Jeeves to know about the kidnapping. It would be too hard to explain without finally letting Jeeves in on Uncle Runyon's line of work. She crept silently up the drive past him and then slithered up the stairs to the house. Once inside, she ran upstairs to find Uncle Runyon's bedroom, prepared to wake him, but he was propped up on pillows, looking pale and ill. He was reading a magazine and seemed only mildly surprised to see her.

"Madeline, dear," he said when she burst in. "What are you doing here? Or am I imagining you? My fever keeps spiking. Still, why imagine *you*? Why not imagine a big piece of pie instead? I have nothing against you personally, but I have to say, I prefer pie." He closed his eyes and tried to change her into pie, but he could not. She still stood before him, berryless and devoid of whipped cream.

Madeline ignored this departure into pie and gave him an organized and coherent account of events before handing him the note.

"Extraordinary," he murmured. Then he sighed. "Still, I do think you'd make a better piece of pie. Banana cream, maybe. Or any pie of your choice. I'm willing to give you some lati-

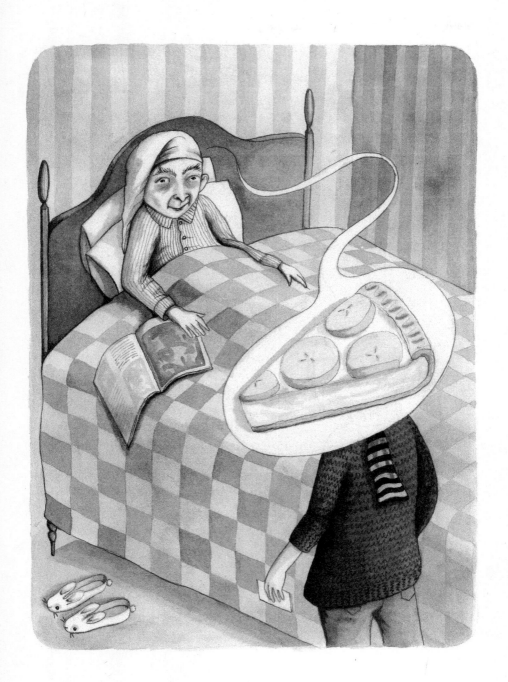

tude on that. You don't suppose you could make more of an *effort* to be pie? Do something for a sick old uncle?"

"Uncle, honestly."

"No cake, though. I'm not a fan."

"Please."

"It's the texture, I think. Too dry."

"I am not interested in morphing into dessert, especially not now, with Flo and Mildred in trouble. In fact, even without their predicament. I am never going to be pie. Have you got that? NEVER PIE!"

"No need to shout."

"I'm sorry you're ill, but you ought to think about Flo and Mildred. If you want pie, tell Jeeves to bring you pie. That's what he's here for, isn't he?"

"You know, I've never been entirely sure *what* Jeeves is here for. Some people, well, *most* people just seem to show up in your life with no clear purpose. Have you noticed that? They're like dust mites. You know they're *there*, you just don't know what to do about them."

"Maybe we can talk about this sometime when no one has been kidnapped. Could you read the note again? I can't help feeling you didn't quite take it in."

Uncle Runyon read the note once more and sighed. He stared at the ceiling, and Madeline thought he was finally on track and thinking of what must be done, when he suddenly said, "Do you think that's a spider up there or an ant?"

"UNCLE!"

"Hmmm? Oh. Right." He sighed again. "You know, all these years I have been living in a fool's paradise. I really didn't think anyone cared about me or what I did."

"Of course they do," said Madeline reassuringly, even as she thought that surely now was no time to have to prop up his flagging ego. "I'm sure every enemy nation cares very much about what you do. You're the only decoder scientist in Canada!"

"Not the only one, dear, just the best," corrected her uncle. "But even as the best, I ask myself, what difference have I made in the world? Sunday night on *60 Minutes* there was the most fascinating show about a woman who has spent her life studying the language of elephants. She is ready to compile an elephant dictionary. You know, you hear more and more of these stories, scientists finding out that birds not only speak to each other but they use syntax. Of course, I have always suspected that animals had sophisticated languages, but most people just don't notice these things. They think animals are grunting mindlessly. But more and more we find certain humans who can speak the language of the animal. Horse whisperers, dog whisperers."

"Oh yes," said Madeline. "I've heard of those."

"And now scientists suspect there are certain humans who can speak all animal languages. Think of it! To understand Bird and Deer and Cat! Why, the questions we could ask! The things we could learn! Those scientists haven't found the person who can do so yet, but it is clearly only a matter of time. They have found all kinds of language aptitude in the brains of the dog whisperers. And why not? Communication is all energy! Energy! Everything is energy!"

"Calm down," whispered Madeline hopefully.

"How can I calm down? It's fascinating! Now, *those* scientists have done something worthwhile with their lives. Einstein believed that an underlying reality existed in nature that was independent of our ability to observe or measure it."

"Yes, yes, that's all very interesting," said Madeline, who was torn. It *was* interesting. She *would* like to learn more about it. But not *now*. "But it's not really the point, is it? Flo and

Mildred have been kidnapped because someone wants to get to *you*."

"Yes, but why would anyone want *me*? Little old me?" Uncle Runyon assumed what he thought was a humble expression, but it only succeeded in making him look like a deranged basset hound.

Madeline took two steps back in alarm and then rallied.

"Who cares!" she wailed. "It doesn't matter why they want you. Once they figure out that Flo and Mildred have brains the size of lima beans, they are going to come back to the island to ask *me* where you are and I am going to *tell* them. Otherwise they might hurt Flo and Mildred. I just came to warn you so, you know, you can hide or something. And I was silly enough to think that maybe you would come up with a plan to help me save Flo and Mildred."

"Oh, my dear, by the time they come for you they will have already disposed of Flo and Mildred, no matter what they tell you. Don't you ever read thrillers?" asked Uncle Runyon.

"WHAT?"

"Not a fan? What do you like to read, dear?"

"*Pride and Prejudice* and . . . what difference does it make?"

"Well, to begin with, no one gets kidnapped in *Pride and Prejudice*. No help for you there."

"Uncle!"

"Oh, no doubt you've learned how to negotiate hunky men who ignore their dates, but for practical advice I think we need a writer like . . . hmmmm, Lee Child, perhaps. Now, he could instruct you that as soon as the kidnappers figure out Flo and Mildred can't help them, that's it for the poor dears. Kidnappers rarely keep the victims around. You can't blame them, really. All our houses are so uselessly cluttered, even without a bunch of bodies in the basement."

"Uncle!"

"I burn things, but still, it's hard to keep up with the clutter."

"Uncle!"

"You're safe here with me, but you mustn't go *home*, Madeline. That's the last place you should go. You can't help Flo and Mildred *there*. Only by us piecing together where your parents might be and getting to them before the enemy gives up interrogating them can you save Flo and Mildred."

"Yes, that's what we need to do. Let's make a plan. Let's think."

Uncle Runyon stared with great concentration at the ceiling. At last he said, "You know, I think I have it."

"YES?"

"It took me the longest time to determine."

"That's all right. Just spit it out."

"I think it *is* a spider!"

"Oh, Uncle, that really is the last straw. I'm giving up on you. I'm getting Jeeves. Maybe he can help."

At this, Uncle Runyon seemed to come fully awake. "No, no, no, no, no, no, no! We mustn't get *Jeeves*! We must never tell *Jeeves*!"

"Why not?"

"Oh, my dear, it's soooo hard to get good help. You really do have to coddle them, insulate them from any kidnappings or murders you might be engaged in. I mean, I don't even tell him when the drains get clogged."

"Well, how are we ever going to find this enemy?" asked Madeline. "All you can find are spiders."

"Yes, but it's a start. Stop frowning at me like that. Let me think," said Uncle Runyon. "My brain is fuzzy. I'm not well, you know. Pneumonia. My doctor said I'm just a heartbeat away from a coma."

"Oh, Uncle!" said Madeline. "That's terrible. Not to mention very inconvenient."

"Oh, it's not that bad. I'm just itching to have a coma, truth be told. I've heard they're very refreshing."

"Well, for heaven's sake, don't have one now," said Madeline. "There's work to be done. Maybe we should start with the police."

"I really wish you had read at least *one* thriller. If the kidnappers say you can't go to the police, you really can't. I suppose I could call Ottawa, but that would take such time. Even getting requisition forms for paper clips takes weeks. I can't imagine how long it would take for them to approve some actual human help. They might not even believe us. Of course, we might get a few extra paper clips out of it."

"Paper clips!" said Madeline.

"Don't say it like that. Paper clips *hold things together*. I've far more idea what they're doing in my life than Jeeves. I mean, I know there are people who go in for staples, but in my estimation, you can't beat a good paper clip. Now, what we need are clues. If we only had clues! I'm afraid we're going to have to rely on you for those, since I wasn't there. I was here busy working on my coma."

Clues, thought Madeline. What had she seen?

"Oh!" she said suddenly. "This will sound ridiculous, but I was almost run over by a car when I was walking home. It had blackened windows but out of them seemed to be looking dozens of red eyes. And I could swear I saw a fox driving. I know that's crazy."

"Oh no, fascinating. Wait a second! That could be my niche! Plenty of people studying the language of animals, but who is studying their *driving skills*? Eh? Eh?"

Madeline stopped wringing her hands obsessively and took a closer look at her uncle. He seemed to be slipping over the edge. Perhaps he wasn't just being eccentric. Perhaps he was delirious. It was one thing to be Einstein and believe in nature's underlying reality. It was another to be her uncle and believe in nature's driving skills.

"Yes, we must find these foxes, not just to get your parents back but to begin my research! That's it. I've made my decision. I'm done with this decoding nonsense. I'm going to do something meaningful with the rest of my life. I'm going to study comparative steering among species. How do deer negotiate roundabouts, as opposed to, say, chipmunks?"

"Oh, Uncle, let's get you some more Tylenol," said Madeline. "Maybe we can pack you in ice until you make sense."

"No time, it's after the foxes we go!" said Uncle Runyon, struggling out of bed.

Madeline pushed him back into it. "You mustn't get up. You're delirious with fever. You're crazy, you're—"

Uncle Runyon, who had taken hold of her sweater to steady himself, ended up with his hand in her pocket in an effort to keep his balance, and in doing so, he pulled out the file card that Madeline had found and forgotten about.

He sat back on his pillows and read it. "Aha! Fanny Fox's Canned Rabbit Products and By-products. By God, they're not just driving, they're running factories! There's a Nobel Prize here somewhere!"

"Oh, Uncle, really, it's probably just some lady with the last name of Fox. Where's your Tylenol?" Madeline was frantically searching the bedside table while her uncle read the file card.

"Very interesting—it's in code," he said. "Of course, that's why they wanted me. They wanted me to decode this. And really, I don't see why, it's just a r . . ." And with that, Uncle Runyon fell backward on his pillow.

"Uncle!" cried Madeline. "Uncle!"

But it was no good. Uncle Runyon had finally fallen into the coma he had been itching to have.

Madeline had the foresight to pick up the note and the file card before racing down to get Jeeves. He seemed as startled by her presence as by her announcement of Uncle Runyon's coma, but like the faithful and good manservant he was, he didn't voice his surprise. Instead, he telephoned the doctor, who came and confirmed Uncle Runyon's coma. The doctor promised he would send a nurse to stay at the manor house. Then Jeeves readied a guest room for Madeline.

Madeline went to it gratefully and sank into bed. It was three a.m., and she was too tired to try to think of what she must do next. She watched out the window as the last embers from the extinguished bonfire drifted up into the heavens. Flo and Mildred had never gotten themselves into a situation that she hadn't been able to fix. Would she wake up tomorrow stymied by this one? Or perhaps wake up to find out it was all a dream. Or that she was merely completely insane. That would be a *huge* relief, she thought crankily. Or maybe I'll just have a coma. That seems like a popular option. She thought of Flo and Mildred with their jewelry making and candle burning and penchant for being kidnapped and Uncle Runyon with his spider watching and comas. *Grown-ups!* she thought. And then she fell asleep.

MR. AND MRS. BUNNY
BECOME DETECTIVES!

"Mr. Bunny, I have had *an idea*!"

Mr. and Mrs. Bunny were sitting in the back garden of their new house, enjoying the fine summer morning and watching the smoke rise from some fire on the horizon.

"Do tell," he said.

"I think we should become detectives."

"That's it?"

"Yes."

"What about my job with the carrot marketing board?"

"Quit."

"And your job collecting lint and creating art from it?"

"That is not a job, that is a calling. But to heck with it. Let's go buy fedoras."

Mr. Bunny grimaced. He suspected that many of Mrs. Bunny's sudden enthusiasms were just thinly disguised excuses to go shopping. But he knew better than to bring this up.

"Detective licenses?"

"I think fedoras are enough. Anyone who sees a bunny in a fedora will not feel the need to see a license."

"It is very hard to find fedoras with holes cut out for our long and fuzzy ears, Mrs. Bunny. On the other hand, if we go to town we can drive our bright and shiny red Smart car."

The car, as you will recall, had been included in the sale of the house, but so far the Bunnys had had no occasion to try it out.

Mrs. Bunny frowned. She had reservations about such a vehicle herself. For one thing, Mr. Bunny was a little too fond of going around the house pretending to shift gears and murmuring "Zoom zoom" in a loud and speeding way. She shuddered to think what he would do when he finally got his long and floppy foot on the gas pedal. Secondly, Mr. Bunny didn't know how to drive. She felt sure this was going to be a problem.

"Mr. Bunny, I think we could use some exercise. Let us leave the car for another day."

"Nonsense, you've been hopping around that garden all morning. You're hopped out. What we need is a pleasant summer morning drive. Zoom. Zoom."

"I knew it," muttered Mrs. Bunny to herself.

By the time she had her purse and shawl and had locked the door against the possibility of foxes, Mr. Bunny was already behind the wheel, looking flummoxed.

"I just don't get it," he said when Mrs. Bunny got in. "What makes it go?"

"What have you tried?"

"I have sat here saying all the car-starting sounds I could think of, including 'zoom zoom' and 'zuppety zuppety,' which always makes *me* go, Mrs. Bunny, but the car has not gotten the idea."

"Maybe it has an On button. Like a light switch."

"Please, Mrs. Bunny," said Mr. Bunny. "Don't display your automotive ignorance. That is a particularly ridiculous idea."

"Well, then, what is that slot there?"

"Where?"

"On the side of the steering wheel."

"That's . . ." Mr. Bunny studied it furiously from all angles. "That's where you keep your parking coins."

"I don't believe a coin would fit in there," said Mrs. Bunny. "Unless it was a very bendy-shaped coin."

"Would," said Mr. Bunny.

"Well, I can be of no more help."

"You could get out and push," said Mr. Bunny. "I'm fairly certain if you pushed and I steered we could get this thing to town in very little more time than it would take to hop. Particularly when you factor in going down hills. Of course, at the bottom of the hills I would have to wait for you to catch up and you would have to hop very fast so as not to keep me waiting."

Mrs. Bunny's answer to this was to get out and start hopping down the road. She trusted Mr. Bunny would catch up when he was in his right mind again. And indeed, shortly afterward, who should hop up behind her but Mr. Bunny himself.

And then all was silence until an hour later, when, drenched in sweat (merely misted in the case of Mrs. Bunny), the Bunnys found themselves on Main Street. Rabbits abounded. All hopping. All shopping.

"Have you ever seen so many bunnies in one place at one time?" asked Mr. Bunny.

"And not a shotgun in sight," said Mrs. Bunny. "It's like a bunny miracle."

But Mr. Bunny did not seem to be paying attention, until Mrs. Bunny poked him, and then he said, "Mrs. Bunny, as I live and breathe! Look! Across the street." He pointed.

"Oh, Mr. Bunny!" cried Mrs. Bunny. "A hat shoppe!"

And then she poked him again. Not because he wasn't paying attention but because when she did it the first time she found she liked it.

Mrs. Bunny might think she was getting away with this, but Mr. Bunny was silently counting the pokes to pay her back later.

The Bunnies hopped up and opened the door, which caused a little bell at the top of it to tinkle. Mr. Bunny had never come across a tinkling door before. It startled him so much that he fell against a display of bonnets and it was lilies, lilies everywhere.

A proprietress bunny came hopping quickly from behind a counter and extricated him. "Oh, I am so sorry," she said.

"No, I am so sorry," Mr. Bunny said gallantly, although privately he thought people who attached bells to their doors got what they deserved.

"Not at all," said the proprietress, picking beads and feathers out of Mr. Bunny's fur. "It does have a startling effect, I find, on bunnies who have just come up from the country and have never heard a shoppe bell. Trust me, you are not the first to find yourself splayed among the hats."

Mrs. Bunny bristled at this. She did not want to be thought of as a country bunny, true though it might be.

"*I* was not at all startled," she said. "All the best shoppes have bells. Some even have *whistles.*"

"Really?" said the proprietress. "I have never heard a whistling shoppe."

"Oh? Pity."

The proprietress was busy picking the last of the sequins off poor befuddled Mr. Bunny. He surveyed the wreckage he had caused and decided that since he would be no good putting things back in their proper places, he needn't even try.

Mr. Bunny's conscience was always extremely easy to placate. It was what he liked best about it.

"Anyhow," said Mr. Bunny, "we have come looking for fedoras."

"Ah," said the proprietress. "Then you are shopping for yourself, sir?"

"Yes," said Mr. Bunny, who did so like being called sir. "And a fedora for Mrs. Bunny too."

"Really?" said the proprietress. "The fedoras are kept, you see, in the men's section."

"Perhaps," said Mrs. Bunny, "that is because such a small nonwhistling town is too tiny to support a fedora-wearing female bunny population."

Mr. Bunny and the proprietress stared at her blankly.

"I'm sure you're right, whatever you said," said the proprietress. "Well, let me show you what I've got. It isn't much, I must warn you. It might not suit such urbane bunnies as yourselves."

And Mrs. Bunny could swear there was the merest hint of sarcasm in the proprietress's tone. It made Mrs. Bunny want to deck her.

"Oh, Mr. Bunny," said Mrs. Bunny in excitement when the proprietress had hopped to a hat rack where several fedoras of different size and color were arranged. "They have *earholes*!"

"You have only seen earholeless fedoras?" asked the proprietress. "Perhaps then your last town was a *human* one?"

Mrs. Bunny paled. She had been found out! She wasn't an urbane bunny after all. She was just another country bunny who had lived on the outskirts of a human town. There was no lower status amongst bunnies.

Mr. Bunny, as usual, was clueless. He was busy examining fedoras. "These are remarkably smooth and comfortable. They look freshly brushed too," he said admiringly.

"Yes, I belong to a hatters' club, and we do all the upkeep on the hats. We are not a hat shoppe that just lets our hats sit around gathering dust. We take good care of them until they find a happy home on top of some fuzzy head," said the proprietress.

"A hat club!" exclaimed Mrs. Bunny, despite herself. "Oh, how wonderful! To belong to such a thing! You must be the happiest bunny on earth!"

"You are welcome to join," said the proprietress. "We are always looking for new members. We are not such a popular club as you might think, even though our refreshments are of the best carroty sort."

"Oh, Mr. Bunny! To join a club on my first day in town!" squealed Mrs. Bunny. "This is so kind of you. Mr. Bunny, I would like the white fedora, if it's all the same to you."

"No good," said Mr. Bunny.

"Why not?" asked Mrs. Bunny, who had put it on and was admiring herself in the mirror.

"I think she looks very charming in it," said the proprietress.

"Yes, but it stands out. A detective does not want to stand out. We need plain brown fedoras that will blend in with our fuzzy ears and whiskers and not shout out 'Detective on the premises!'"

"I beg to differ, Mr. Bunny," said Mrs. Bunny, who was growing more attached to the white hat by the minute. "Any fedora at all is sure to scream out 'Detective on the premises!' That is, in fact, the point of the fedora."

"Perhaps," said Mr. Bunny. "But you don't want it to shout out 'Detective too stupid to even *try* to disguise herself!' now do you, Mrs. Bunny? Particularly when you are supposed to be *undercover*."

And Mrs. Bunny had to allow that one did not, and so she put back the lovely white hat and handed two brown ones to the proprietress, who rang up the purchase. While Mr. Bunny fumbled with his bills and coins, Mrs. Bunny said, "Tell me, is there a fire beyond the village? From our cottage we seemed to see one in this direction."

"Oh, that comes from the manor house. We don't know what they burn or why. Indeed, our newspaper reporters would like to do a story about it, but of course they are too timid to go on the grounds. So they just write stories in which they speculate. Occasionally when they tire of this they make things up."

"That sounds like fun. Let's become reporter bunnies," said Mrs. Bunny to Mr. Bunny.

"One short-lived enthusiasm at a time, Mrs. Bunny," said Mr. Bunny, handing over the correct change. "For now it sounds to me like what this town needs is a pair of detecting bunnies on the case."

"Well, good luck," said the proprietress. "Now, Mrs. Bunny, do come Friday to the hat club meeting. We meet in this very shoppe. Bring a carrot cake."

The Bunnys said their goodbyes and hopped back outside.

"I do not like being told what kind of cake to bring," said Mrs. Bunny.

"Never mind that, Mrs. Bunny," said Mr. Bunny, happily donning his brown hat and handing Mrs. Bunny hers. "Our first detecting job! The Case of the Large Amount of Smoke."

"Hmm," said Mrs. Bunny, eyeing the brown hat thoughtfully. Then she hopped back inside to exchange it for the white one after all.

THE CASE OF THE LARGE AMOUNT OF SMOKE

"So, Mrs. Bunny," said Mr. Bunny as they hopped over their thirty-third hill. "Don't you wish we had taken the car?"

"Yes, if it came with a driver," muttered Mrs. Bunny under her breath. Indeed, she had very little breath left to mutter with. "Are you sure we are going in the right direction? I do wish you had let me stop and get a map."

"Nonsense. All we have to do is hop toward the manor house."

"Yes, but *have* we been hopping toward it?" panted Mrs. Bunny. "It feels to me like we're hopping around in circles. I'm sure we've been up this hill before."

"Oh, be quiet, Mrs. Bunny."

And then Mrs. Bunny, who was hopping ahead of Mr. Bunny, saw a great lump on top of a hill. It looked like someone sitting with a blanket over her head, but this seemed such a ridiculous thing to do at the crest of a hill with a lovely view on a beautiful summer morning that Mrs. Bunny decided she must be wrong.

"Mrs. Bunny," said Mr. Bunny, "I wish I had a Nerf bat. Do you remember Guess That Lump?"

When the baby Bunnys were small, Mr. and Mrs. Bunny had entertained themselves by letting them hide under blankets and hitting them with the Nerf bat, saying in loud, theatrical tones, "WHAT'S THAT LUMP?" It was endlessly amusing but not apt to have the same effect with strangers, Mrs. Bunny feared.

Nevertheless, Mr. Bunny was willing to give it a try with a poke from a stick in place of the Nerf bat, when suddenly a head popped out and a little girl looked at them blankly.

The Bunnys were used to being looked at blankly. It was seldom a human tried to make eye contact.

"WHAT'S THAT LUMP?" shouted Mr. Bunny anyway, just for the heck of it.

It had a very strange effect. The little girl actually seemed to understand. She gave Mr. Bunny a look of pure terror and went immediately back under the blanket.

Madeline sat quietly waiting for the bunnies to go away. She had been sitting under the blanket all morning. When she had awoken and checked on Uncle Runyon, she'd found him still in his coma. After eating the breakfast Jeeves prepared for her, she had gone outside to try and figure out which things that had taken place the day before had been real and which had been imagined. She had almost decided that she herself was not insane, merely mistaken about the foxes, when the bunnies accosted her. Now she had to rethink. Between this and trying to figure out how to find her parents, her brains were becoming terrifically overworked. She poked one eye out from a corner of the blanket. Yes, there were talking bunnies there, all right. The one in the brown fedora was saying, "For all the world, as if she understood what I said!"

"Oh dear, Mr. Bunny, but if she did, you must have frightened her terribly, shouting 'What's that lump?' at her."

"It must be a coincidence," said Mr. Bunny. "You know humans never understand Bunny language. Maybe she's just afraid of rabbits."

"I think you may be a hallucination," said Madeline from under the blanket.

"The idea! That *we* could be a hallucination. If anyone's a hallucination, it's you!" said Mr. Bunny.

"Right back at you," said Madeline through the blanket. She wasn't usually so rude, but it was okay to be rude to imaginary bunnies.

"Right back at you again!" said Mr. Bunny.

"Are you going to repeat everything I say?"

"Are you going to repeat everything I say?" said Mr. Bunny.

Madeline whipped the blanket off and said, "What is the *matter* with you?"

"That's a very good question," said Mrs. Bunny, trying to pat Madeline reassuringly on the ankle. But it only made Madeline scooch rapidly backward until she lost her balance and rolled down the hill.

"I am always asking myself what is the matter with Mr. Bunny," Mrs. Bunny called after her in a friendly manner.

Madeline thought that maybe if she lay very still it would all go away. Stress, she thought, it's the stress. She *was* losing her mind. That was the only possible explanation for the talking rabbits and driving foxes. The thing to do was to calm down. KatyD had taught her self-hypnosis during the lulls at the café in the rainy months when there were never many customers. She had taught Madeline self-hypnosis, Reiki, tae kwon do, and a little Serbo-Croatian, but only the self-hypnosis had stuck. Even though she had never used it before, Madeline remembered what to do. The idea was to think of a place that relaxed you, so Madeline imagined walking through a field on Hornby. She took deep calming breaths. She imagined it in detail. The flowers. The butterflies. The fluffy clouds. She began to feel slightly better.

Now that I am calm, they will have disappeared, she said to herself, and opened one eye. The Bunnys were still there. They had followed her down the hill and were bent over, giving her worried, inquiring looks.

"I think I'll just go for a walk now, and *then* maybe I'll stop hallucinating," Madeline said.

"For the last time, you are *not* hallucinating," said Mr. Bunny.

"Never mind hallucinating; do you *live* in the manor house?" asked Mrs. Bunny excitedly.

"Um, why else would I be here on these grounds?" asked

Madeline, hedging. She didn't feel like going into the long explanation of what she was doing there.

"We don't live here and we are on the grounds," said Mrs. Bunny. "Of course, we didn't know until you mentioned it that we were on the manor house grounds. We *wanted* to be on the grounds, but mostly we were hopping in circles. Because Mr. Bunny wouldn't let me buy a map."

"We were not hopping in circles. I knew exactly where we were going. Your sense of direction, Mrs. Bunny, is all in your—"

"So, you were coming to the manor house on purpose?" interposed Madeline tactfully.

"Yes, to detect!" said Mrs. Bunny.

"You're not supposed to tell people that," said Mr. Bunny.

"Oh," said Mrs. Bunny, and bit on a knuckle. "I forgot."

"Detect what?" asked Madeline.

"What and why you are burning things!" said Mrs. Bunny. "We're detectives!"

"MRS. BUNNY! You have more enthusiasm than brains."

"I'm not burning things," said Madeline. "That's my uncle's butler."

"Isn't he your butler too?" asked Mr. Bunny.

"Actually, I'm just visiting," said Madeline.

As they watched from afar, they could see the butler carrying boxes to the fire. He upended them, and a blizzard of old socks hit the flames. Smoke filled the air, and a wind blew it toward them.

Oh, honestly, Uncle, thought Madeline, old socks?

"Is that burning legal?" asked Mrs. Bunny. "It smells very polluting to me."

"I don't know," said Madeline. "Suddenly I don't seem to know what's what about anything."

"I'm sure you know lots of things, dear," said Mrs. Bunny. "How long are you visiting your uncle?"

"I don't know that either, he's deathly ill," said Madeline.

"You poor dear. Your uncle is deathly ill and your parents are"—and here Mrs. Bunny bent down to whisper tactfully— "dead."

"DEAD!" said Madeline, completely hysterical now. "What do you know that I don't know?"

"NOTHING!" said Mrs. Bunny, falling over backward in alarm.

"Then why would you *say* that?" asked Madeline, sitting

up and bending over Mrs. Bunny in a frighteningly crazy manner.

"Whoa, whoa, whoa," said Mr. Bunny, hopping between them. "It was a natural assumption."

"Why? What do *you* know?" asked Madeline breathlessly, dreading the worst.

"Well . . . ," said Mrs. Bunny.

She and Mr. Bunny exchanged glances.

"You see," said Mr. Bunny, "we've never talked to a human before, so really, all we know of them is from books."

"We read a lot of books. Children's books mostly, because they're always much more truthful than adult books. And much more entertaining," said Mrs. Bunny.

"And in all of them," said Mr. Bunny.

"With few exceptions," said Mrs. Bunny.

"The parents are dead," they finished together.

"Oh," said Madeline. "Well, they're not dead, they're just . . ." And then she stopped. One of the things she had been trying to decide was whom it would be safe to tell about her parents. It was clear she was going to need some help finding them. If these rabbits were real, then foxes might indeed have been the ones to kidnap Flo and Mildred. In which case, stumbling upon a pair of detectives, even rabbit detectives, was the most fortuitous thing that could have happened to her. She reached into her pocket and pulled out the six dollars she had left. She held it out to Mrs. Bunny. "Is this enough to hire a detective? I mean, if I was going to."

"Well, dear, first I think we need to discuss the case," said Mrs. Bunny, trying to remain calm but practically falling back *up* the hill in excitement. Their first client!

"Yes," said Mr. Bunny. "We must proceed in a businesslike fashion. Put that back in your pocket and follow us."

Madeline's stomach growled. With all the flurry of activity and adrenaline in the last two days, she was starving. Breakfast seemed like a long time ago. Mr. and Mrs. Bunny averted their eyes politely.

"Why don't you come to our hutch for lunch, dear? It's just over those thirty-seven hills. Hopping, hopping, never stopping, that's our motto," said Mrs. Bunny.

The prospect of thirty-seven hills was not a welcome one at the moment, but as she started walking, Madeline discovered that there was a certain point in fatigue where it was possible to keep moving one foot after another with little thought to what came next.

The Bunnys came up from behind her now and then and gave her a helpful shove. They said they were tired from their busy day too, and so everyone was very happy when the hutch came into view.

"Scones!" said Mrs. Bunny.

"Tea!" said Mr. Bunny.

"Anything at all!" said Madeline as she followed Mrs. Bunny toward the doorway of the hutch.

"And you can tell us where you learned to speak Bunny," said Mr. Bunny.

"Learned to speak Bunny?" said Madeline in surprise. "But I don't. I thought you were speaking English."

"We can *understand* English," said Mrs. Bunny. "Although we can't yet speak it very fluently."

"We speak Fox, Marmot, Bird," said Mr. Bunny. "You know, the Romance languages. All bunnies learn those in grade school. Later we might pick up a little Bear. Some Groundhog, a touch of Prairie Dog."

"Highly esoteric," sniffed Mrs. Bunny. "And impractical. I keep telling him he should take a course in Squirrel."

"But humans never understand Bunny. Not without being taught. Unless . . ."

They both stared at her wide-eyed, although she could only see Mrs. Bunny. Mr. Bunny was still behind her, outside.

"She's a . . . ," began Mr. Bunny.

"Bunny whisperer!" said Mrs. Bunny in awed tones.

"Are you?" asked Mr. Bunny.

"I don't know," said Madeline, who had frozen in the doorway like a statue. "I mean, if I am, I never knew it. Of course, no bunnies have ever spoken to me before."

"In general, dear, we like to be spoken to first," said Mrs. Bunny.

"Well, since I've never *learned* Bunny, I guess I must be," said Madeline.

"Extraordinary," said Mrs. Bunny.

"Not as extraordinary as it would be if a human finally took the time to actually learn *our* language instead of expecting *us* to speak *theirs*," said Mr. Bunny.

"Now, now, let's not get political, she's just a little girl," said Mrs. Bunny. "So, Madeline, tell us what is bothering you so."

"It's hard to know where to begin—" Madeline said.

"Of course it is," Mrs. Bunny interrupted soothingly as she put a paw on Madeline's arm and gave her a helpful tug forward. "Come in and have a nice cup of tea to loosen your lips."

"I can't," said Madeline, wiggling helplessly in the doorway. Her eyes filled with tears. Did everything have to go wrong? "I'm stuck."

MR. AND MRS. BUNNY ARE HIRED

"Yes, I thought that the first second I saw you. I didn't raise twelve rabbits for nothing. Well, that's what tea is good for," said Mrs. Bunny. "You sip it and find a way to tell us."

"No, not stuck as in I can't find a way to express myself, or stuck as in a problem, stuck as in the *door*!"

"Nonsense," said Mr. Bunny. "Give yourself a push."

Mr. Bunny was on the outside and Mrs. Bunny was on the inside and Madeline was wedged tightly in the door frame with her neck at a very uncomfortable angle.

"I tried. I can't move. I'm telling you, I'm stuck!"

"Well, this won't do. You're blocking the doorway so I

can't get in either. I want my tea too," said Mr. Bunny. "Did you think of that?"

"I didn't do it for fun," said Madeline.

"Well, come back out, then," said Mr. Bunny.

"I can't," said Madeline, tearing up again.

"We shall have to push her," said Mr. Bunny. "Heave ho, Mrs. Bunny."

Mr. Bunny pushed from the outside. Mrs. Bunny pushed from the inside. It was quite some time before Madeline realized that they were pushing against each other and that was why she was going nowhere.

"Oh, I *am* tired," said Madeline. "I can't think straight. Stop pushing, both of you."

"It's not our fault. For such a little girl you certainly have a big bottom," said Mr. Bunny.

"I'm always telling him not to say things like that," Mrs. Bunny whispered to Madeline. "He always thinks people won't take offense."

"I don't know how to get myself out of this doorway without knocking out one of your walls with my feet," said Madeline.

"Well, don't, for heaven's sake, do that," said Mr. Bunny.

"Oh dear, this is a disaster," said Mrs. Bunny. "And I was going to treat you to my carrot scones with carrot jelly."

"Mrs. Bunny, your brains are clearly fried from too much hopping. Her mouth is, after all, on your side. You could serve her a scone with jelly while we try to figure out how to move her humungous bottom."

"I'd be afraid to," said Mrs. Bunny. "She might just blow up and get stuck all the more. I think what we will have to do is starve her out."

"I'm already starving," said Madeline.

"That's true. She's already starving, Mrs. Bunny, and you can see what good it's done. No, I shall simply have to go for my crowbar."

"Mr. Bunny is a wonder with a crowbar," Mrs. Bunny whispered to Madeline.

"Why are you whispering?" asked Mr. Bunny.

"I don't know," said Mrs. Bunny. "It just seems a comforting way to talk to someone who is stuck."

Mr. Bunny hopped off to the toolshed and returned with his crowbar.

"This may smart a little," he said.

Madeline closed her eyes and braced herself. Then she

realized that she must unbrace herself or she'd never get out. Mr. Bunny did his crowbar magic and with a few sharp tugs had Madeline out of the doorway and back in the garden.

Mrs. Bunny came out. "Well, I think we can congratulate ourselves on our good fortune."

"And excellent crowbarmanship!" said Mr. Bunny. "Now we'll have tea in the garden. And we won't say another word about Madeline's humungous bottom. It will be lovely outside on such a fine day."

Mrs. Bunny hopped in to get the victuals while Mr. Bunny led Madeline to the iron table and chairs. Unfortunately, although the table was suitable, the chairs were all too small for her.

"That big bottom again," said Mr. Bunny, forgetting his promise.

"I don't have a big bottom!" protested Madeline. "You have small chairs."

Mr. Bunny just shook his head sadly. Many people were in denial about their large bottoms.

Fortunately, at that moment Mrs. Bunny hopped out with the tea tray, and although the scones and cups of tea were bunny, not people size, Madeline found that by drinking several potfuls of tea and eating platefuls of rabbit-sized scones, she was quite as satisfied as the Bunnys with this repast.

I *definitely* could not have imagined *this*, she thought. Maybe I *am* a bunny whisperer. And Uncle was right, the things you could find out if you could speak an animal's language! For instance, how many people knew that there were rabbit detectives?

"So," Madeline began. "As I said, I might need to hire some detectives."

"At your service," said Mr. Bunny.

"Likewise," said Mrs. Bunny. "And really, I don't think we can even charge for it. We do a certain amount of pro bono work, don't we, Mr. Bunny?"

"Tons, tons and tons of pro bono work," said Mr. Bunny.

"What's that?" asked Madeline.

"I really don't know," said Mr. Bunny.

"It means we don't charge," said Mrs. Bunny.

"Oh, well, thank you. Now, um, Mr. and Mrs. Bunny—" Madeline began.

"Yes? For so we are called," interrupted Mr. Bunny.

"Just out of curiosity, how much detecting have you, um, done?"

"Oh, lots. Tons. Oodles," lied Mr. Bunny enthusiastically. "Some pro bono, some anti."

"We solved the Case of the Large Amount of Smoke in a trice," said Mrs. Bunny.

"Have you ever looked for, um, say, something living?" asked Madeline.

"Of course, we *could* branch out to people," said Mrs. Bunny.

They looked at Madeline inquiringly.

Madeline thought about this. They seemed very silly, and they were bunnies, but they were the only detectives she was apt to come across any time soon. "Okay, you're hired. Well, it all started on the day of Luminara. I had just found out Prince Charles was coming to our school, and I went home to tell Flo and Mildred—"

"Are we going to find Prince Charles?" the Bunnys shouted together.

"No, no, but he's coming to our school, Comox Elementary, and I wanted to go to the ceremony because he will be giving out awards and I won some but I don't have white shoes. . . ."

The Bunnys nodded sagaciously, as if she were making any sense.

"Of course you must go to the graduation! Prince Charles! My, my!" said Mrs. Bunny.

"Then you know who he is?" asked Madeline. She somehow was surprised that rabbits knew such things.

"Oh yes. After all, we're Commonwealth rabbits," said Mrs. Bunny. "But you must get some white shoes."

"Yes, I know, but I couldn't because Flo and Mildred—"

"Who are Flo and Mildred?" interrupted Mr. Bunny.

"Oh. My parents. Flo and Mildred—"

"For so they are called," said Mr. Bunny serenely.

"Didn't want me to get white shoes. That is, there was no money for them. So I waitressed and I had the money and then, well, they didn't want me to anyway, of course . . . but that's neither here nor there and not important now and not why I hired you."

"No indeed, but it could be a case in itself. The Case of the White Shoes. You say you needed some for the ceremony—"

"Yes," said Madeline, feeling silly because Flo had pointed out how superficial the whole thing was. "You see, my teacher—"

"Oh, no need to explain, dear," said Mrs. Bunny hurriedly. "My goodness, I had twelve bunnies of my own. Your teacher wanted everyone dressed alike for the prince. Well, that's only natural. Oh, how I miss these events now that the bunnies are grown and gone. Christmas concerts, graduations, fun fairs."

"Since time is short, let's not waste any more of it. We'll worry about the shoes later. Tell us about the case," said Mr. Bunny, leaning forward.

"Well," said Madeline. "This is probably going to sound ridiculous, but it looks as if my parents were kidnapped by f—"

"FIENDS!" Mrs. Bunny had the unfortunate habit of finishing people's sentences.

"Fillains!" said Mr. Bunny, who couldn't think of an *f* word but wanted to join in the game.

"Fairies!" said Mrs. Bunny.

Madeline was beginning to regret hiring them. "Foxes," she said.

The effect of this word was far more dramatic than she expected. The Bunnys' playful expressions vanished. Under their fur she could see them turning pale. Their very ears quivered.

Madeline passed them the kidnappers' note and the file card.

"This is grave," said Mr. Bunny.

"Very grave," said Mrs. Bunny after she had read both. "Oh, Mr. Bunny! Rabbit by-products!"

"This is evil. It's impossible to know if such a factory exists yet. I hardly think it does, because there would be far more rabbits disappearing. But whether it is a factory that is just being built or this is just some fox's idea of a joke, we cannot know. Nevertheless, whatever it is, we must put a stop to it. But why would they want your parents? And what are all these confounded squiggles on the file card?" asked Mr. Bunny.

So Madeline explained about her uncle and how the foxes obviously needed him for decoding.

"We must get on the case immediately. We must find your parents before the foxes, uh, get hungry, and we must find out if such an evil factory has already been built and, if it has, run those foxes out."

"How will you do that?" asked Madeline.

"Oh, we have a special antifox SWAT team, but before the Bunny Council will send them out, we must know where the foxes are. There have been too many false alarms when bunnies only thought there were foxes about. It's a form of bunny hysteria. Now the council makes you present solid evidence."

"And fill out ninety-three requisition forms," said Mrs. Bunny.

"That's why Uncle didn't want to call Ottawa," said Madeline. "The requisition forms. He said we must solve this mystery ourselves, and we were about to when he fell into his coma."

"Very bad luck there," said Mr. Bunny, clucking his tongue.

"But good luck to have found us," said Mrs. Bunny.

She and Mr. Bunny put on their fedoras and spent the rest of the afternoon pacing the garden, trying to think of what to do next. They were very disappointed to find that sporting fedoras, while fashion-forward, did nothing to inspire their detecting brains.

Periodically Madeline would call out, "Do you have an idea yet?" and Mr. Bunny would reply, "Shhh, patience, you must give the fedora time to work."

In the end, Mr. and Mrs. Bunny had not an idea between the two of them, but they did not want to tell Madeline this. They could see that what she needed most was hope.

"Don't worry," said Mr. Bunny. "The germ of a seed of a spore of an idea begins. We must let it grow overnight."

"Really?" said Madeline. "That *does* sound promising."

"Yes, it does, doesn't it?" said Mr. Bunny, feeling pleased with his big fat lie. "Dinnertime approaches. We would invite you to stay with us, but, of course, you won't fit into the guest room."

"So perhaps we should all rejoin after my hat club meeting tomorrow," said Mrs. Bunny as she headed into the house with the dirty cups and saucers. "Now, we should escort you home so you can get some rest. Tomorrow will be very busy."

What a long day it has been, Madeline thought. I can hardly stand the thought of those thirty-seven hills. Then she noticed the Smart car in the driveway.

"You have a car!"

"We *have* a car," said Mrs. Bunny, coming out and wringing her paws. "We just don't know how to start it."

"We don't know how to start *this* kind of car," said Mr. Bunny.

"Well, I've seen KatyD start hers lots of times before," said Madeline. "Give me the keys and I will see if I can show you what she does."

"Keys?" said Mr. and Mrs. Bunny.

"The car keys," said Madeline.

The Bunnys looked at her blankly.

"You need keys to start a car. The keys go into this little hole right here on the side of the steering wheel."

"Oh, I hope there's room for them, what with all the parking coins," said Mrs. Bunny, giving Mr. Bunny a look.

"Do you know where the keys are?" asked Madeline.

"No, you see, we inherited the car with the house," said Mrs. Bunny.

"Well, in my experience people quite often keep them hanging on a hook in the front hall," said Madeline.

Mrs. Bunny hopped into the house and came back out right away with a set of keys hanging from one paw. "Exactly where you said they'd be!"

"You would make a fine detective, Madeline," said Mr. Bunny. "If we could just find some way to disguise your gigantic bottom."

"Do you think you could show Mr. Bunny how to start the car?" interrupted Mrs. Bunny hastily. "And also how to drive it?"

"Didn't he have to learn before he got his license?" asked Madeline.

"Bunnies don't need licenses," said Mr. Bunny. "They are

born with a certain innate knowledge of all things worth knowing. Hand me the keys, please."

Mr. Bunny had to sit on six telephone books in order to see out the windshield because the Smart car was a normal human-sized car. Unfortunately, this meant his foot did not reach the gas pedal.

"I have an idea," said Mrs. Bunny, and she hopped back into the house. When she returned she had a pair of twelve-inch purple sequined platform shoes.

"Ah, Mrs. Bunny," said Mr. Bunny, getting out of the car and strapping them on. "A relic of your disco-dancing phase. I knew someday one of your short-lived enthusiasms would come in handy."

Everyone got back in the car. When Mr. Bunny reached down with his newly shod foot, he had no trouble reaching the gas pedal.

Madeline sat in the front passenger seat and politely offered her lap to Mrs. Bunny.

"I could sit happily on the floor," said Mrs. Bunny. "Believe me, the less I see, the better."

"But then you wouldn't fit in the seat belt, and I feel we should definitely wear seat belts," said Madeline.

Mrs. Bunny agreed to sit on Madeline's lap because of the seat belt, but she rode with her paws pressed firmly over her eyes the whole way. Madeline found it comforting to have Mrs. Bunny's warm furry weight on her lap. It reminded her of her younger days with stuffed animals.

Mr. Bunny did not seem to care that he flooded the engine twice; he was clearly having a marvelous time. He braked when he should have applied gas only eleven times and bragged that it must be some kind of record for a beginner. There was no real whiplash, he insisted, that was just Mrs. Bunny exaggerating. By the time they arrived at the driveway to the manor house, Mr. Bunny declared he had things completely under control. Then he ran into the gate. But that could happen to anybody, he pointed out.

Madeline asked Mr. Bunny to let her out there so the butler wouldn't see her.

"Why are you hiding from the butler?" asked Mr. Bunny.

"It's for Uncle's sake," explained Madeline. "Uncle would be thrilled to observe rabbits pulling up in a Smart car. He is going to make it his life work to study your, um, driving habits."

"To each his own," said Mr. Bunny loftily. He felt sure

there was an implied insult in anyone's studying him in any way at all.

"But Jeeves is apparently not to be disturbed with, any, um, disturbing concepts, such as some people might find, um, driving rabbits or kidnapping foxes," finished Madeline awkwardly.

"Don't worry, dear," said Mrs. Bunny, patting Madeline's shoulder, which she could do easily from her position on Madeline's lap. "Good help is so hard to find. In fact, don't worry about a thing. Mr. Bunny and I have everything under control."

Mrs. Bunny, having thus reassured twelve children of her own in days gone by, had quite the knack for it, and Madeline found herself feeling greatly comforted. Nobody had ever reassured her about anything, and it was a wonderful novel sensation. She went inside, had dinner and went happily to sleep.

But after Madeline had gone, Mrs. Bunny turned to Mr. Bunny and said, "I have no idea what we're doing, have you? I mean, usually I don't mind having no idea what we are doing, but now I feel we really must. We're going to have to step it up, Mr. Bunny."

"Don't worry," said Mr. Bunny resolutely. "Already I suspect someone. I consider that half the battle."

"Whom do you suspect?" asked Mrs. Bunny.

"The butler."

"How so?" asked Mrs. Bunny. "I thought it was foxes who were to blame."

"No doubt they have co-opted the butler," said Mr. Bunny.

"But then they would know where the uncle was," said Mrs. Bunny reasonably. "They wouldn't need to kidnap Madeline's parents."

"And yet I feel we must still suspect him in some capacity. In every detective novel, is it not the butler who did it? They always announce it out of the blue at the end. But here's where we have the jump on them. We are suspecting him from the first!"

Mrs. Bunny sighed. When Mr. Bunny got ahold of an idea, he did not like to let go of it. And even when he did let go of it, he pretended he hadn't. This whole idea of the butler was completely ridiculous, and now she would have to hear about him until the end of the case. She sighed again.

"And I think we'd better get Madeline to stay with us," continued Mr. Bunny. "She may be in danger even at the manor house if her parents suddenly remember where her uncle lives."

"But the foxes won't care about Madeline at that point. It's the uncle and his decoding skills they want."

"Unless they go on a fox rampage. You know how horrible that can be."

Mrs. Bunny shuddered. "I hadn't thought of that. But where will she sleep?"

"Tomorrow when you're at your meeting, I shall bring her back to the hutch and we will build her a guest cottage just her size."

Mrs. Bunny nodded. "I'll leave out some beet salad sandwiches for you. And cupcakes. Children love cupcakes."

"Mr. Bunny loves cupcakes," Mr. Bunny reminded her, and then stepped on the gas, causing Mrs. Bunny to clamp her paws back over her eyes, which Mr. Bunny thought very unsporting of her. Until he realized that it gave him an excellent opportunity to give her the two swift pokes he owed her.

⫸THE CODED MESSAGE⫷

With a good day's detecting work under their belts, the Bunnys were enjoying their nightly routine in their new hutch. Mr. Bunny had found an armchair and reading lamp by the living room fireplace that he declared an excellent fit. The old owners' subscription to *The Scientific Bunny* hadn't been canceled, and Mr. Bunny enjoyed reading choice nuggets of it to Mrs. Bunny while she knitted. He informed her of archaeological digs in search of ancient rabbit life, and the latest in genome phenomena (Mrs. Bunny usually tuned him out and thought about the garden during this), and now he was happily settled reading a very long article on new things that exploded.

"What, invented just to explode?" asked Mrs. Bunny. "That seems very wasteful to me. Why would you want to invent something to explode?"

"Science marches on, my dear," said Mr. Bunny. "Sometimes a man just wants an exploding item around. And the things that exploded last year are old news. Listen to what they have developed to explode in just the last month: phenohepteroids—"

"I beg your pardon?"

"It's an alkaloid of some kind," said Mr. Bunny knowledgeably.

"The things you know, Mr. Bunny!"

"I like to keep up," said Mr. Bunny. "Books with the word *pfeffernüusse* in the title."

"They explode?"

"Exploding all over the place, apparently."

"Do they warn people?"

"Doesn't say. They've developed an exploding variety of prune plums. *That's* a shame. I like prune plums . . ." Mr. Bunny would have gone on reading the list, but there was a knock on the door.

"A visitor! Our first visitor, Mrs. Bunny. I hope he brought cake!"

Mrs. Bunny opened the door. It was Mrs. Treaclebunny from across the way. She was a widow who lived alone in a tiny cottage on her own large meadow across from the Bunnys. The Bunnys were quite envious. Mrs. Treaclebunny had an ocean view.

"How do you do," said Mrs. Treaclebunny. "I have been waiting for an opportune time to come and introduce myself."

"Delighted," said Mrs. Bunny. "Do come in."

"Oh, mustn't intrude, mustn't intrude," said Mrs. Treaclebunny, coming in and sitting down in Mrs. Bunny's chair by the fire. "My name is Mrs. Treaclebunny."

"Yes, so we gathered from your mailbox. We've seen you hopping about too, of course. Meant to say hello," said Mr. Bunny. "I am Mr. Bunny, and this is Mrs. Bunny."

"Charmed," said Mrs. Treaclebunny, and then no one could think of anything else to say.

Finally Mrs. Treaclebunny said, "Well, now that we're old acquaintances of several minutes' standing, I feel I might ask you a favor."

"Anything at all," said Mrs. Bunny, relieved that someone had found something to say.

"Yes. I came over to see if I could borrow a cup of toilet bowl cleaner." Mrs. Treaclebunny held out a teacup she had brought for this purpose. "I was cleaning the bathrooms and found I'd run out and I didn't feel like hopping all the way into town just for that."

"Well, of course," said Mrs. Bunny, taking the teacup and hopping into the bathroom to fill it. She handed it back to Mrs. Treaclebunny, expecting her to rise and depart. After all, who wants to sit around all evening holding a teacup full of toilet bowl cleaner? But Mrs. Treaclebunny didn't stir.

"I was also wondering if you had any spare dinner about?" said Mrs. Treaclebunny.

Mr. Bunny threw Mrs. Bunny a look.

"Uh," said Mrs. Bunny. "We may. I made a stir-fry so there's never *very* much left. It is one of Mr. Bunny's favorites."

"It *is* Mr. Bunny's favorite, and he was counting on the leftovers for a little midnight snack," said Mr. Bunny, none too subtly.

"I'm *very* hungry," said Mrs. Treaclebunny.

"Oh, of course, in that case," said Mrs. Bunny, and, not knowing what else to do, hopped into the kitchen, heated the rest of the stir-fry in the microwave, brought it back to Mrs. Treaclebunny, held the teacup of toilet bowl cleaner for her and watched her devour the stir-fry.

"It could do with some fresh ginger," said Mrs. Treaclebunny when she was done. "Thanks very much. See you."

She took back the toilet bowl cleaner and hopped out without another word, spilling drops of it here and there on her way.

"Honestly, Mrs. Bunny," said Mr. Bunny. "Is this what you were pining for, living on the mountainside without bunnies all those years? Neighbors? Is this what you had in mind? I'm going to bed. Will you be coming too or waiting up to see if anyone is in need of deodorant and drain cleaner?"

"Humph," said Mrs. Bunny, who didn't think much of Mr. Bunny's sarcasm when it was directed at her. She countered it with a dignified flounce. She flounced all to pieces. Then, flounced out, she headed up to bed.

The next day Mrs. Bunny made carrot cakes until she baked one she deemed worthy to bring to the hat club meeting.

Mr. Bunny told her she was becoming an obsessive cake maker and he hoped it wasn't the beginning of other odd habits.

"How you do run on and on," said Mrs. Bunny dismissively while knitting winter underwear out of used dental floss. She had greatly reduced their carbon footprint that year doing this alone. Suddenly she had an idea. She put down her underwear knitting pattern and turned the pages of her knitting book until she found what she wanted. Then she started a whole new knitting project with a smile on her face.

Finally, it was time for Mrs. Bunny's hat club meeting. She carried her cake out to the car, put it carefully on the floor and then put her paws firmly over her eyes as Mr. Bunny drove her to the hat shoppe.

After Mrs. Bunny got out, he drove on to the manor house to collect Madeline, who was waiting by the gate.

"How is your uncle?" asked Mr. Bunny.

"He's still in a coma," said Madeline.

"That's dreadful," said Mr. Bunny. "Gosh, I hope he doesn't die!"

"Well, that's not very tactful!" wailed Madeline. "Is that supposed to make me feel better?"

"Oh dear, I'm afraid not. If Mrs. Bunny were here she

would stuff a sock in my mouth," said Mr. Bunny, looking remorseful. "I'm sure he won't die. Don't worry. I had a coma once for three years and woke up very refreshed. Mrs. Bunny even suggested to a travel agency that they offer bargain vacations along those lines. The ad campaign could read, CAN'T AFFORD THE BAHAMAS THIS YEAR? TRY A COMA!"

"THREE YEARS!" said Madeline. "If we can't find Flo and Mildred ourselves, we'll need Uncle out of his coma and decoding that file card sooner than that. I'm sure there must be a clue there. A clue that starts with *r*. I need more time to brainstorm such things with you, so I thought maybe we could put up a tent for me at your hutch. I already told Uncle's butler I was going to stay with the Bunnys. I think he may have thought that was the last name of someone human. Well, of course that's what he thought. And you see, this way we can devote all our energies to the search."

"Our idea exactly. Except we thought you and I should spend the morning building you a guest cottage while Mrs. Bunny is in her hat club meeting."

"Isn't that a waste of time? Wouldn't a tent be easier and quicker? I really think we need to find Flo and Mildred *soon*!"

"I think if the plan is to drag Mrs. Bunny out of the first

club meeting she has ever gone to, it is going to take more than two of us," said Mr. Bunny, looking speculative.

"Oh, all right, but I hope it won't be a *long* meeting," said Madeline, nervously twisting the corner of her shirt.

Mrs. Bunny's hat club meeting was a howling success. There was some milling about and chitchat before it began, and Mrs. Bunny was quite the social maven.

Then the proprietress, whose name was Mrs. Ruskeebunny, started the meeting by saying, "I have the most wonderful idea! Next week is the annual parade of bonnets. We had planned to be hopping down Main Street as usual. *However,* I have just overheard some news that could change everything! Mrs. Bunny has been telling Mrs. Hopbunny that Prince Charles is coming to Comox Elementary! Suppose we take the parade to Comox? To hop in front of the school as the prince arrives? What greater honor can we rabbits bestow upon him than to grace him with our bonnety presence?"

There was a great buzz of excited noise as the ladies considered this.

"All in favor say 'Aye,'" said Mrs. Ruskeebunny.

It was unanimously decided to go.

"Excellent. Then we will hire some Greyhound Explorers," she began.

There was a shrill shriek from the back. "Greyhounds! Run for your lives!"

"Thank you, Mrs. Sneepbunny, but not all greyhounds are dogs. Some of them are buses."

Several bunnies had fainted, but Mrs. Ruskeebunny paid no attention. There were always a few drama queen bunnies.

"And thank you, Mrs. Bunny, for bringing us this wonderful information. And at your very first meeting!"

There was a rousing round of applause. Mrs. Bunny blushed and blushed.

"Now, we must make our bonnets extra-special. As you know, in years past we have lined the bonnets with silk, but if it rained, our furry heads got drenched. So this year it has been suggested that we make our bonnets more weatherproof. To this end I have purchased several rolls of plastic lining, and I shall show you how to attach it to the hats."

"Won't that cause dreaded furry head sweating?" asked

one of the members. Her husband was a furatologist and saw many cases of this when bunnies overhatted.

"Not at all," said Mrs. Ruskeebunny. "In my experience only the gentleman bunny sweats. The lady bunny dews, at most. And dewing is very attractive. No, I think we should line all the bonnets with plastic this year. It will be expensive but will protect the bunny's head from rain. We don't want to greet Prince Charles looking like a bunch of drowned cats! And next week it may be rainy."

"Very rainy," said Mrs. Bunny.

"Very, very rainy," said Mrs. Tobagobunny.

"Very rainy," said Mrs. Sneepbunny.

It was hard to tell if they were all agreeable or just unoriginal. It hardly mattered to Mrs. Bunny, of course. She was having a *marvelous* time. She even told them about her lint art, and they exclaimed that she must bring some in to show them *for sure*.

So she was feeling elated, until Mr. Bunny picked her up. One look at his face and she forgot her happy morning in a trice. "Why, Mr. Bunny," she said as they pulled away from the curb, "whatever is the matter?"

"We must hurry and get back on the case. Madeline and

I built a cottage for her, and I brought in a team of plumber bunnies, who installed a small bathroom. I'm afraid to even look at the bill."

"Oh, money," said Mrs. Bunny. If Mr. Bunny was merely having a conniption over expenses, she need not be concerned.

"Let us not be so cavalier about the bills. But that's not the problem. Madeline is just in a *state* about these parents of hers. We must rescue them *now*, she keeps saying. We are taking too long. She has been practically hysterical. And *what* parents they turn out to be! While we built the cottage, Madeline told me dreadful tales. As you already know, she is made to waitress for shoe money. But wait! It gets worse! Her parents won't even come to her parent-teacher conferences. She goes in their place. They completely refuse to attend her Christmas concerts and graduation ceremonies. *She* is the one who changes the lightbulbs in her house! It sounds to me like *she* takes care of *them*."

"Oh, Mr. Bunny!" sobbed Mrs. Bunny.

"Yes," said Mr. Bunny with satisfaction. You could always tell when you'd told a heartrending tale well because Mrs. Bunny could not control the waterworks. There were damp puddles on the seat already. You could water crops with Mrs.

Bunny's tears once she got going. Indeed, Mr. Bunny had often thought of holding her over the lettuces.

They drove a bit in silence and then Mrs. Bunny said, "You know, Mr. Bunny, maybe we could . . . uh . . ."

"We could what?" asked Mr. Bunny, still thinking about how well he had handled it all.

"Keep her," said Mrs. Bunny in high, strangulated tones.

"Oh, Mrs. Bunny, we're not supposed to befriend humans, let alone adopt them."

"No? Then I think we must steal her," said Mrs. Bunny, mulling it over.

"Mrs. Bunny, get ahold of yourself."

Mrs. Bunny said no more, but she still thought it was a good idea.

In the meantime, Madeline was pacing.

When she saw the Bunnys' car pull up, she ran to it.

"Finally!" she said. "Let's go find Flo and Mildred."

"Let's have some soup first," said Mrs. Bunny reasonably. "It's no good detecting on an empty stomach."

Mrs. Bunny had vowed to herself that from now on somebody was going to take care of Madeline. This was going to be her priority. Even before finding Flo and Mildred and closing down the evil factory.

"I can't help feeling everything is taking too long. You said you had things under control, but we haven't done anything! Maybe we should see if we can get a doctor to *force* Uncle out of his coma. Do you think that would be possible?"

"Not if he is enjoying himself," said Mr. Bunny. "People can be very stubborn about remaining comatose. No, the first thing to do is to try to decode the note ourselves. Let us have the soup while we do it. No one can decode with a malnourished brain."

Madeline set the outside table, and Mrs. Bunny heated up some soup, and the three of them slurped soup and worked on the note.

They read it frontways and backways and upside down. Mrs. Bunny suggested they try reading it while standing on their heads, and though that didn't seem to make any sense, they tried that too. It didn't help.

Mrs. Bunny said that inspiration was sure to strike at any

second. Mr. Bunny then remembered his secret decoder ring that had come in a box of Carrotloop cereal. He went inside to get it. But that didn't work either.

"Oh dear, oh dear, oh dear," said Madeline.

"Would you like some more soup, dear?" asked Mrs. Bunny.

"She doesn't want more soup, she wants her note decoded," said Mr. Bunny. "There's only one thing to do, and I had hoped to avoid it."

"Oh no," said Mrs. Bunny. "Don't even think it."

"What?" asked Madeline.

Mr. Bunny sighed. "We shall have to visit a marmot."

⊨THE MARMOT⊨

"**N**O!" said Mrs. Bunny. "NOT MARMOTS!"

"What's so terrible about that?" asked Madeline.

Mr. and Mrs. Bunny laughed and laughed.

"What's so funny?" asked Madeline. They didn't look as if they were having fun, they looked hysterical.

"Nothing," choked out Mr. Bunny between guffaws. "It's just *too terrible* to think about."

"What do they do that is so awful?" asked Madeline.

"When they come to visit, they don't bring cake," said Mr. Bunny.

"I came for a visit and I didn't bring cake," said Madeline.

There was an awkward silence.

"But you're family. You need *never* bring cake," Mrs. Bunny said hastily.

Madeline felt a faint glow. Then she thought, my adopted family are rabbits. I finally fit in somewhere and it is with a whole different species. Naturally.

"But there is one marmot talent that, while usually pretty useless, is of the greatest value to us right now."

"They can decode," said Mr. Bunny. "They can decode like sons-of-guns."

"Virtual Rosetta Stones, every one of them," said Mrs. Bunny. "And the greatest one of them all, the one who has never been stumped, is The Marmot."

"The marmot? Which marmot?"

"That's his name. His parents named him The, and of course his last name is Marmot. So he is The Marmot. And *that* should tell you all you need to know about marmots, even if you didn't already know about the cake thing," said Mrs. Bunny.

"But we have to find Flo and Mildred!" said Madeline. "So can't we forget about the cake thing temporarily?"

"Temporarily," said Mr. Bunny.

"Because it really is *so* rude," said Mrs. Bunny.

"Yes," said Madeline. "Now, where do we find The Marmot?"

"Well, that's another thing," said Mr. Bunny. "You never know about marmots."

"They keep changing their houses. One day they're here. One day they're there."

"They're very transient," said Mr. Bunny.

"And they don't bring cake," said Mrs. Bunny.

"Yes, yes, we've covered that," said Madeline impatiently. "Well, how do we find out where The Marmot lives, then?"

Mr. and Mrs. Bunny looked at each other.

"We thought all children knew how to find things," said Mr. Bunny.

"Google," said Mrs. Bunny.

"I didn't know you could Google marmots," said Madeline.

"You can Google anything, dear," said Mrs. Bunny patronizingly. "I just learned how to use the computer this year. Mr. Bunny taught me."

"And I'm never teaching you anything again," said Mr. Bunny.

"You got that straight," said Mrs. Bunny.

"Well, what are we waiting for?" said Madeline, so Mr. Bunny hopped inside to his computer and Googled The Marmot.

He came out waving a piece of paper with the address, and the three of them set off over hill and dale to a "particularly ugly part of the countryside," as Mrs. Bunny loftily put it. They pulled up in front of a pile of dirt.

"Look at that hole he lives in," said Mrs. Bunny scathingly.

"Shhh," said Madeline. "That's not nice."

"Not *nice*?" said Mr. Bunny. "It's just *accurate*. Marmots live in holes."

"Mr. Bunny," Madeline began. They were there begging favors. He needed to be tactful.

"Yes? For so I am called," said Mr. Bunny.

"But there are holes and *holes*," interrupted Mrs. Bunny, sniffing.

"They don't even plaster. They don't put floors down. They don't paint. Dirt floors, dirt walls, that's good enough for them," said Mr. Bunny.

They got out, getting rather muddy in the process, for it had started to rain and marmots also don't keep proper lawns or gardens, drives or walkways, so the Bunnys were up to their furry knees in mud.

"There's not even any place to knock," said Mrs. Bunny.

"If it were me, I'd install a nice ground-level doorbell," said Mr. Bunny speculatively.

"Hello, Mr. Marmot!" Madeline called down the hole.

"*Mr.* indeed," said Mr. Bunny. "Hey, you big marmot head, answer your door, why don't you!"

"Be nice," said Madeline. "Or he won't want to come out."

Just then a furry face with teeth that protruded a bit too much to be attractive poked out.

"Well? What do *you* want?" asked The Marmot. "It's not often we get bunnies in these parts. Not visiting *us*. Not often. And humans? Humans who speak Marmot? Never."

"You see," whispered Mrs. Bunny to Madeline. "Can't even make intelligent conversation."

"Mr. Marmot, I'm pleased to meet you," said Madeline. Then she stopped. "Are we speaking Marmot or Bunny now?"

"A little bit of each, dear," said Mrs. Bunny.

"I understand *both*?" said Madeline. An exciting thought was occurring to her. Was she one of the people scientists were looking for who could speak all animal languages? She knew she was smart. She had, after all, read *Pride and Prejudice.* Twice.

But she didn't know she was *that* smart. No, smart wasn't really the word for it. It was a gift. Was she so gifted?

"She doesn't even know what languages she is speaking? What a dummy," said The Marmot.

"Shut up," said Mr. Bunny.

"This is Madeline," interjected Mrs. Bunny hastily. "And she is certainly no dummy. You remember me and Mr. Bunny. We've come on an errand of grave importance."

"You need help digging a grave, is that it?" asked The Marmot. "Someone told you marmots were good diggers, did they? Well, we are, we are, we are. Look at this lovely hole I've dug. Come to the right place, you have. Cost you a million dollars, but I'll take the job!"

"A million dollars! You idiot marmot!" roared Mr. Bunny, but Madeline put a restraining hand on his shoulder.

"No, it's your superior intelligence we're after," she said soothingly.

"Oh, that, oh, that, oh, that," said The Marmot. He closed his eyes a minute to let the meaning of this come to him. Then he said, "Okay, I don't know what you mean. Better come in and explain. Talk slowly and repeat things several times."

The Marmot turned and went back into the hole. Mr. and Mrs. Bunny looked at Madeline and rolled their eyes.

"Mrs. Bunny and I can come in," called Mr. Bunny down The Marmot's long echoey hole.

Come in come in come in echoed back.

"He must have a very long hallway leading down to his living room," said Mrs. Bunny.

"But Madeline can't!" shouted Mr. Bunny. CAN'T CAN'T CAN'T echoed back up the hole. "Because she's got such a gigantic bottom!" GIGANTIC BOTTOM, GIGANTIC BOTTOM, GIGANTIC BOTTOM.

"Please don't," whispered Madeline. It was one thing to have this said about you and another to have it echoing back from the earth like a fundamental truth.

"Yes, that's enough of that," said Mrs. Bunny, pushing Mr. Bunny back from the hole's edge. "You're going to traumatize her. Now listen, Marmot, get back up here. We can't stand in the rain and we can't come down the hole, so we're going to have to find a tea shoppe or someplace Madeline can fit into to have our chat. We don't want to go to a human one, though. We'd end up being on the menu."

"Even if you weren't," said Madeline, "I can't bring two rabbits and a marmot into a tea shoppe."

"Well, then we'll have to go to Rabbitville and find a restaurant large enough to accommodate you," said Mrs. Bunny.

"The Olde Spaghetti Factory!" said Mr. Bunny.

"Oh, Mr. Bunny, you are a smart rabbit!" said Mrs. Bunny.

"Oh, I love The Olde Spaghetti Factory," said Madeline.

Once, on a mad gay vacation, her parents had taken her to a real motel and The Olde Spaghetti Factory. Everyone was having a marvelous time until Flo found out that the restaurant was using nonunion lettuce. They had to leave in the middle of their meal, but Madeline had never forgotten it. It was the only vacation they had ever been able to afford and it had been just wonderful until the salad course. "I didn't know that rabbits had one."

"Rabbits have everything," said Mr. Bunny.

"And everyone has The Olde Spaghetti Factory," said Mrs. Bunny.

The Marmot poked his head out of the hole. "Did I hear someone say The Olde Spaghetti Factory?"

So Mr. Bunny hopped back into the driver's seat, Madeline put both The Marmot and Mrs. Bunny on her lap and they rode into town with Mrs. Bunny holding her nose the whole way.

"Why, your Olde Spaghetti Factory is exactly the same size as our human one!" said Madeline in surprise when they pulled into the parking lot.

"They're exactly the same all over the world. It is part of their charm," said Mr. Bunny. "Now listen, Marmot, we're going to have to disguise you. We can't, obviously, bring a marmot in here. They might possibly tolerate a human, but no one is going to let in a marmot."

"Meatballs, cannelloni, garlic bread," said The Marmot, drooling and licking his lips.

"Right," said Mr. Bunny, clamping his fedora on The Marmot's head. Mrs. Bunny found a spare pair of sunglasses in her purse, and Madeline took off the scarf she had around her neck. It was too big, of course, but they wound it six or seven times around The Marmot's neck until even his own mother wouldn't have known him.

"Mr. Bunny, you are a master of disguise," said Mrs. Bunny admiringly.

"Yes, it is one of my many talents," said Mr. Bunny with satisfaction. "Come!" And he led the way into The Olde Spaghetti Factory.

The Marmot tripped six or seven times due to his dark glasses and the restaurant's dim lighting.

"Stop calling attention to yourself," said Mr. Bunny.

"I can't help it," said The Marmot. "Get a booth. Oh! And get some crayons and menus to color with."

"Can I have a children's menu and some crayons?" said Madeline when the waiter came. Madeline took up four chairs, but Mr. Bunny, with great self-restraint, didn't mention it.

The waiter placed a child's menu and crayons in front of Madeline. The Marmot nudged Mr. Bunny in the ribs.

"And another set for my marmot," said Mr. Bunny, almost giving away the show.

But Madeline and Mrs. Bunny agreed that this remark had gone right over the waiter's head. After the waiter brought the crayons, The Marmot began scribbling away for all he was worth.

"Look, I can stay in the lines!" he said to the waiter.

"Shut up," whispered Mr. Bunny.

Then The Marmot ordered the most expensive thing on the menu.

"What did I tell you?" said Mrs. Bunny to Madeline, raising her eyebrows.

"Let's get down to business," said Madeline, clearing her throat.

She handed The Marmot the coded file card. At first, he put it on the table and picked up a crayon. He was about to use it when Mr. and Mrs. Bunny and Madeline all shouted "NO!"

"Just decode it, please," said Mr. Bunny when they had all calmed down.

"Hmmmm," said The Marmot, looking at the file card. "Very interesting. Very interesting indeed. I wonder what rabbit by-products are." He looked pensive.

"Would you just decode, please?" said Mr. Bunny through clenched teeth.

The marmot sat and studied the code as they made their way through gigantic plates of pasta. The Marmot ate all the garlic bread in the basket and called for three refills.

"We're going to have to pay for that, you know," said Mr. Bunny to Mrs. Bunny.

"It's for a good cause, dear," said Mrs. Bunny.

"It doesn't even occur to him that *others* might like a little garlic bread," said Mr. Bunny, sniffing.

"Well?" asked Madeline as the waiter took the plates away and brought them dessert menus.

The Marmot ordered the most expensive dessert, which was baked Alaska, and then he ordered Irish coffee too.

"You know Irish coffee *is* a dessert," said Mr. Bunny. "So you've just ordered *two* desserts. And did you know there is whiskey in Irish coffee? And this is lunchtime. I'm just saying."

"It helps me think," said The Marmot, going back to studying the coded card, and no one said anything after that.

The Marmot grabbed all four after dinner mints that the waiter brought, and still no one said anything.

"WELL?" said Mr. Bunny finally, when he was paying the bill and The Marmot was loading his pockets with free toothpicks from the container by the cash register.

"I'll tell you what I think," said The Marmot.

"YES?" they all cried.

"I think that this card is in *code*," said The Marmot. "And . . . by the way, where's the restroom?"

Mrs. Bunny pointed down the hall to the doors with

restroom signs. One showed a bunny in trousers and the other showed a bunny in a skirt.

"Which one do I use?" asked The Marmot.

"*This* is who we have decoding for us?" said Mr. Bunny.

Mrs. Bunny pointed to the sign with the bunny in trousers and The Marmot scurried in.

The Bunnys and Madeline sat on a bench by the restaurant door and waited for The Marmot to return. They waited and waited. Finally Mr. Bunny hopped down the hall to the restroom to see what was keeping him. When Mr. Bunny returned he looked flummoxed.

"Well? Has he fallen into the toilet? This sometimes happens with marmots," Mrs. Bunny said, turning to Madeline.

"No," said Mr. Bunny. "Worse."

MADELINE HYPNOTIZES
A MARMOT

Madeline and Mrs. Bunny stared at Mr. Bunny blankly. What could be worse than falling into a toilet? Madeline thought it would certainly be the low point of *her* day.

"He's disappeared," Mr. Bunny said.

"Impossible," said Madeline. "How could he? There's no back way out. You can see where the hallway ends."

"He's got the only copy of the coded card with him," said Mr. Bunny.

"Where could The Marmot have gone? Think, Mr. Bunny," urged Mrs. Bunny.

"Let's go outside and see if we can't find him," said Madeline.

"He *did* have that Irish coffee," said Mrs. Bunny. "Maybe it went to his head and he left by the window accidentally."

"No one leaves by a window accidentally," said Mr. Bunny.

"You're right. There are more sinister forces at work," said Mrs. Bunny.

"Sinister, my elbow," said Mr. Bunny. "Marmot forces at work is more like it."

The three rushed out to the parking lot and did a complete circuit of the restaurant, but there was no sign of The Marmot.

"Not only that, but he made off with my fedora," said Mr. Bunny. "Now I shall have to detect bareheaded."

"Maybe he just forgot about us and went home," said Madeline. "Let's check there first."

They ran back to the parking lot, but now they realized that the Smart car was gone too.

"SWELL! That tears it! I left the keys and my driving shoes in the car and now he's stolen it!" said Mr. Bunny.

"What shall we do?" asked Madeline, sitting down with a thump, followed by the two thumps of Mr. and Mrs. Bunny.

They sat on the curb for sixteen minutes in a state of complete despair.

"Well, it will cost a fortune but I suppose we will have to call a taxi," said Mr. Bunny finally.

"Rabbits have *taxis*?" said Madeline, leaping to her feet.

"I told you rabbits have everything," said Mr. Bunny.

So Mr. Bunny went inside and phoned a taxi. He asked for one large enough to accommodate a really gigantic bottom.

The taxi driver arrived shortly and took them to The Marmot's hole. While the driver waited, the Bunnys ran over to the hole entrance and Madeline cased the grounds.

"I've found the car!" she called. "It's over here behind this rock pile."

"You come out of there, you dirty thief!" yelled Mr. Bunny down the hole. "We know you stole our car."

"I didn't steal nothing," The Marmot called back. "Go away, I'm trying to sleep."

"You come up or I'll come down and drag you up," said Mr. Bunny. He was so mad his fur was standing on end.

A very sleepy-looking marmot dragged himself out of the hole.

"What did you think you were doing, stealing our car and running away like that?" asked Mr. Bunny.

"I wasn't stealing nothing," said The Marmot. "I just should never have had that Irish coffee. It got me all confused."

"Didn't I warn you that that would happen?" demanded Mr. Bunny, and went to pay the driver.

When he returned, it was to hear Madeline shout, "YOU DID WHAT?"

"Oh, honestly, I knew we never should have started up with marmots. It's always a mistake," said Mrs. Bunny, hopping in circles and pulling at her fur.

"What? What did he do?" asked Mr. Bunny.

"He *lost* the file card," said Madeline.

"HE *WHAT*?"

"Lose it? Did I lose it? That's the question," said The Marmot.

"Do you have it now?" asked Mr. Bunny

"Noooo," said The Marmot, frowning in perplexity.

"Then that's the answer, you idiot. Now think, *where* did you lose it?"

"That's another question. All these questions after Irish coffee. It's too much. My little marmot brain is bursting. Besides, how can I possibly remember? It was so long ago," said The Marmot. "Before my nap."

"By George, I'll *shake* it out of that marmot brain of yours!" said Mr. Bunny, hopping up and down in place with such force Mrs. Bunny said she was afraid one more hop and he would propel himself right over the moon.

"Calm down, let's think rationally," she said.

"RATIONALLY? THIS IS A MARMOT WE'RE TALKING ABOUT!" yelled Mr. Bunny.

"If there were just some way we could get him to remember!" said Mrs. Bunny.

"Oh!" said Madeline, clapping her hands. "I know! I can hypnotize him. KatyD taught me how. Would you let me do that, Mr. Marmot?"

"Please call me The," said The Marmot affably.

"Uh, all right, The," said Madeline. "Let's all sit here in the, uh, mud, and The, you just relax." Madeline stopped. Her sentences were becoming more and more confusing. "Listen, can I call you something else? Don't you have a nickname?"

"My mother sometimes called me her Special Precious," said The Marmot.

"I don't think I could do that," said Madeline, shuddering.

"Look, just let her call you Mr. Marmot," said Mr. Bunny.

"How about Poindexter?" said The Marmot.

"Why Poindexter?" asked Madeline.

"Please do not ask him questions. Please. We'll be here all night. When it comes to marmots, give orders," said Mr. Bunny.

The Marmot had climbed up a tree and hung upside down by his hind legs, looking perplexed.

"All right, all right. Listen, can I just call you Marmot?" pleaded Madeline, looking up into his puzzled face.

"It doesn't have a very friendly ring."

"All right! *Poindexter*," said Madeline.

The Marmot just hung there.

"Poindexter?" Madeline gently prodded.

The Marmot didn't respond.

Mr. Bunny pinched him. "That's *you*!"

The Marmot fell down from the tree.

"OUCH! I forgot. Keep your paws to yourself, you vicious bunny."

"This isn't going to work," declared Mr. Bunny. "If you're going to concentrate a mind, you need to *begin* with one."

"Let's just take a cleansing breath," said Madeline. "Now,

I want you to begin by thinking of someplace that you find relaxing or something you like to do that relaxes you."

"I like to throw spitballs at robins," said The Marmot.

"YOU LIKE TO *WHAT*?" cried Mr. Bunny in outrage.

"Robins and rabbits have always been allies," Mrs. Bunny whispered to Madeline.

"It's okay, Mr. Bunny, we're not really going to throw spitballs. Only in our minds' eyes. There we are walking through a sunny meadow on a beautiful summer morning. Robins are everywhere. We throw spitballs at them. One spitball, two spitballs, three spitballs . . ."

Madeline tried to give her voice a drowsy soothing tone, and The Marmot's eyes began to close.

"But we don't fall asleep, we just relax. Now, as we're throwing spitballs we think to ourselves about the yummy lunch at The Olde Spaghetti Factory. Sit in that meadow and remember it. You have the coded file card in your hand. . . ."

"It's in my hand," murmured The Marmot drowsily. "I put it down to reach for more garlic bread . . ."

"No, you don't. There is no more garlic bread. You ate it all," said Madeline. "You pick up the file card again."

"I ask Mr. Bunny to order more garlic bread. . . ."

"While you are waiting for it to come, you pick up the file card."

"I pick up the file card."

"You take it into the restroom. . . ."

"I take it into the restroom . . . ," repeated The Marmot.

"And you . . ."

"I put it on the sink and go into the toilet stall . . . ," The Marmot went on.

"The file card is on the sink!" cried Mr. Bunny, hopping up. "What are we waiting for?"

"No . . . ," said The Marmot in the same drowsy hypnotized voice.

"No . . . ," said Madeline, giving Mr. Bunny a look and resuming the soothing tone. "Because . . . what happens next?"

"What happens next is I get into the toilet stall and I think, That file card is too important to leave lying on a sink."

There was a long silence while The Marmot's eyes began to droop.

"The file card is too important to leave on the sink so you . . . ," prompted Madeline.

"So I zip my pants back up," said The Marmot.

"You zip your pants up."

"And I go and get it."

"You go and get it."

"I bring it back with me into the stall . . . ," said The Marmot. "For safekeeping."

"You bring it back with you into the stall. For safekeeping."

"Then I start thinking about the garlic bread again."

"You think about the garlic bread."

"I love garlic bread."

"You love garlic bread. Of course you do. We all love garlic bread," droned Madeline soothingly.

"I wonder if I can get Mr. Bunny to go back and get me several orders to go."

"You wonder if Mr. Bunny will buy you several orders to go."

"Because it would be nice to have some to nibble at night while I watch television."

"Because it would be nice to have some to nibble at night while you watch television."

"But I don't know if Mr. Bunny will go for that."

"But you don't know if Mr. Bunny will go for that."

"He's kind of an ornery bunny, but he wants his file card decoded, so I bet I can get him to do anything."

"Why, you!" said Mr. Bunny.

"Shhh," said Madeline.

"I love garlic bread, so I decide to give it a try," said The Marmot.

"You decide to give it a try."

"I reach for the toilet paper, but the stall I'm in is out of it."

"You reach for the toilet paper, but the stall doesn't have any."

"But then I notice I have a file card in my hand."

"You notice you have a file card in your hand."

"I think, Paper is paper."

"You think, Paper is paper."

"Any old port in a storm."

"Any old port in a storm?"

"So I use the file card."

"You use the file card?"

"Then I flush it down the toilet."

⊁THE DREADED ENVELOPE⊁

"**T**HEN YOU FLUSH IT DOWN THE TOILET?" yelled Madeline.

"YOU IDIOT!" yelled Mr. Bunny.

"Uh-oh," said The Marmot, coming suddenly awake and leaping up. In a flash, he was down his hole.

Madeline closed her eyes. She had entrusted the one thing that might lead her to her parents to a couple of rabbits and a marmot. *She* was the idiot. She picked her way across the scrap heap that passed for The Marmot's front yard and yelled down the hole, "Did you at least *decode* it first?"

"I may have, but I can't talk now. I'm traumatized. And

I'm especially not talking to that hostile rabbit until he's had a chance to calm down. I'm going into my bedroom and *locking* the door," said The Marmot. "It's not my fault I forgot about the file card. You should never have brought me to a restaurant that serves garlic bread."

They heard a door below slam with enough force to shake the ground under their feet.

"It's late," said Mrs. Bunny softly. "Let's go home."

When the Bunnys and Madeline got home, they all had dinner and then the Bunnys put Madeline to bed.

"Don't worry, dear," said Mrs. Bunny. "We'll find Flo and Mildred. Tomorrow is a new day."

"I'm so worried about them," said Madeline. "Suppose they're cold? Suppose Mildred doesn't have enough room to do a downward dog?"

Mr. and Mrs. Bunny looked at each other.

"Just try to get some sleep," said Mr. Bunny, and they hopped back to their own hutch.

Madeline lay shivering in the dark. She had planned to check in on Uncle to see if he was out of his coma, but now there was no rush. Of course, she didn't want him to be in a coma, but even if he came out of it, she had nothing for him to decode. Why hadn't she made photocopies of the file card? She seemed to think of everything too late. Poor Flo and Mildred. She turned the light back on and paced.

"Madeline, turn out your light and go to sleep," called Mrs. Bunny from the hutch.

"I can't," Madeline called back. "I can't sleep in a soft bed when Flo and Mildred might not have one."

"I'm sure The Marmot will remember what he decoded tomorrow. Marmots are like that," called Mrs. Bunny back.

Madeline switched off her light, but she kept pacing restlessly in the dark. She had enjoyed having the support and help of the Bunnys. The problem was, she wasn't used to having anyone taking care of her and making the decisions. It gave her the uneasy feeling that she wasn't doing what she was supposed to be doing. That she shouldn't be trusting so much in the Bunnys' judgment. On the one hand, they were very sweet and responsible adults. On the other hand, they were rabbits. She had to face facts, as much as she didn't want to; if she ever wanted to find Flo and Mildred, at some point she might have to strike out on her own. In the meantime, she would just have to trust that they could cope with whatever came their way. But Oh dear, she thought, who am I kidding? Coping has never been their strong suit.

"I can't cope with this," said Mildred to Flo. They were somewhere in a darkish factory basement, tied back to back. Foxes kept coming in and grilling them about the location of Uncle Runyon, but they simply couldn't remember. Everyone but the Grand Poobah wanted to give up. "I keep telling them I'm a vegan and still they keep bringing animal products. When I asked them why the broth in the vegetable soup was so brown, they said it had a beef base. You see? They just don't get it."

"Hey," Flo called to the guard fox. "You think you could get Mildred, like, a salad or something? You got union lettuce, right?"

The guard looked at him blankly. Just then the door opened and the Grand Poobah entered.

"Oh man, am I glad to see you," said Flo. "This guy, like, just sits there and watches us. It's giving me the creeps. And he won't get Mildred anything. We asked for tofu, a salad,

some peanuts. Like, we're not trying to be a nuisance, man, but she's gotta eat."

"A thousand apologies, my dear dementomando!" said the Poobah, bowing low. He knew that Flo would never guess that it meant "demented man." "But Frederico Fox hasn't learned English yet. He couldn't understand anything you said."

"You've been speaking English?" asked Flo in wonder. "Man, I thought we had just somehow, like, miraculously been understanding Fox. Like those French immersion classes Mildred always wants to take. Where, you know, you just *get* it without having to work at it."

"Mwa-hahaha. Mwa-hahaha," laughed the Grand Poobah. He really did find this most amusing. "I think not. We have been studying English for years now, so that we are, I fancy, rather fluent, for the most part. Fox is far more complicated. You would never learn it."

"Hey, try me, man," said Flo.

"How do you say 'I need something to eat that is *meat-free*!'?" said Mildred.

"*Zakszokeyid,*" said the Grand Poobah. "Now you try it."

"*Je besoin de quelque chois sans viande,*" said Flo.

"That's French," said the Poobah coldly.

"*Geben mir* something mitout the meaties," said Flo.

"That's a combination of German and gibberish," said the Grand Poobah.

"I'm hungry!" said Mildred.

"You will be hungrier still before the night is over. Unless you can remember where your relative lives," said the Grand Poobah.

"Hey, man, we're trying, but nothing's coming. In the meantime, we might as well learn Fox," said Flo. "So we can talk to, like, your guards."

"I would be willing to bet you an, um, say, an earlobe that you cannot learn Fox," said the Grand Poobah, drooling.

"Oh, you're just afraid to find out how much Fox I already understand," said Flo confidently.

"*Zxignsyajhdi,*" said the Grand Poobah.

"What does that mean?" asked Mildred.

"My dear dementoladyo," said the Grand Poobah. "You don't want to know. Mwa-hahaha."

"Hey, maybe if you teach us Fox, it will activate our brains and we'll remember where Runyon lives," said Flo.

"I think not. You're both far too yummy, I mean hopeless," said the Grand Poobah.

"Come on," whined Flo.

"Very well. Repeat after me. *Zadyhenhizsiy.*"

"*La plume est dans ma poche,*" said Flo.

"*Zykidysa.*"

"*Sprechen sie la chêvre.*"

"Where does Runyon live?"

"Hmmm. Can't remember."

"*Zygiofodik.*"

"Still don't remember. But I think I'm beginning to get Fox. That meant summerhouse. Right? Am I right?"

"No. Where's the decoder?"

"Still nothing coming."

And so it went.

All night.

Flo and Mildred didn't learn any Fox or activate their brains enough to remember where Uncle Runyon lived, but the Poobah picked up a little French.

Mrs. Bunny sat knitting next to Mr. Bunny by their hearth.

"I wish she wouldn't worry so much. I'm sure everything will turn out fine. After all, we *are* detectives," she said.

"Of course we are," said Mr. Bunny. "We have the fedoras to prove it."

Mr. Bunny tried to soothe Mrs. Bunny by finishing the article from *The Scientific Bunny* on "New Things That Explode."

"Chicken wings," he read.

"All chicken wings?" asked Mrs. Bunny.

"No, only ones from south Florida. Schzapels."

"What are those?"

"I haven't time to explain," said Mr. Bunny, and then there was a knock on the door.

"What now?" he said. "Don't answer it."

But Mrs. Bunny had already opened the door. It was Mrs. Treaclebunny.

"Thought I saw your light," she said, coming in and sitting in Mrs. Bunny's chair. "Lovely evening."

"It was," said Mr. Bunny.

"Say, do you have any spare toothpaste?" Mrs. Treaclebunny held out her toothbrush.

"I think I have an extra tube in the bathroom drawer," said Mrs. Bunny.

"Oh, I don't need a tube, just squeeze a little on here. Try to make sure it covers all the bristles without slopping over. That's how I like it," Mrs. Treaclebunny said to Mrs. Bunny, who was hopping away to perform this task.

She was some time at it. No matter how hard she tried, she could not get the toothpaste to line up perfectly with the end of the brush. Then she'd have to rinse the brush and start over. It was a disgusting task, rinsing someone else's toothbrush, but Mrs. Bunny thought it her neighborly duty.

When she had finally achieved toothpaste perfection, she came in to find Mrs. Treaclebunny staring at the fire and Mr. Bunny pretending to be asleep in his chair.

"Say, have you got any extra dinner about?" asked Mrs. Treaclebunny, taking the toothbrush.

"Well, I didn't have time to make much," said Mrs. Bunny. "You see, we had a very long and trying day. I just opened a couple of boxes of mac and cheese."

"That'll do," said Mrs. Treaclebunny, so Mrs. Bunny hopped into the kitchen and wearily heated up some of the leftovers. Then she hopped back, gave the plateful to Mrs. Treaclebunny and held her toothbrush while she finished it.

"I'd try adding a little real cheese next time," said Mrs. Treaclebunny. "Perks it up. Well, thank you and good night." And Mrs. Treaclebunny hopped out.

Mr. Bunny's eyes snapped open the second the front door closed.

Then the Bunnys took showers and went to bed.

"It's been a very trying day," said Mrs. Bunny again.

"That is what always happens when you get mixed up with marmots," said Mr. Bunny in the dark.

"I couldn't agree more, dear," said Mrs. Bunny.

Then they reached over and held paws until they fell asleep.

In the morning everyone woke up feeling refreshed and ready to hit the detecting trail.

"I have an idea," Madeline said to the Bunnys when they came in with toast and juice. She had always wanted breakfast in bed, but she couldn't linger over it now; she was too anxious to get back on the case. "Could you make some garlic bread for us to take over to the marmot? To entice him up?"

"What an excellent idea!" said Mrs. Bunny, and made a large batch.

They took it over to The Marmot's hole.

"Listen, you can come out now. No one is mad. We brought you some garlic bread. Mrs. Bunny made it herself," Madeline called down the hole.

"I like the kind from The Olde Spaghetti Factory," called The Marmot.

"Well, perhaps, if you're *very* helpful, we'll get you some from there later," called Madeline.

"I remember things better when I have *real* garlic bread," said The Marmot, but he came up anyway.

"Okay, here's the deal," said The Marmot after he had eaten all the garlic bread and pronounced it decidedly yummy, if inferior to The Olde Spaghetti Factory's. "It's slowly beginning to come back to me. I *did* decode some of the file card before its, uh, unfortunate end. But it's very hard to remember what it said. Somehow that part seems to have all slipped away. Of course, if I had it in front of me . . ."

"Do you think he really *was* traumatized, as he said?" whispered Madeline to Mrs. Bunny. "Don't trauma victims sometimes have trouble remembering?"

"No," sighed Mrs. Bunny. "He's just being a marmot. They're thick as bricks."

"I *do* remember *something*," The Marmot went on.

"Yes?" said Madeline and Mrs. Bunny encouragingly.

"That is, I remember one word I decoded. I know there was more, but for some reason all I can remember is the one word."

"Okay, that's good," said Madeline. "One word is a start."

"What is it?" asked Mrs. Bunny.

"Rubber."

"Rubber?" asked Mrs. Bunny.

"Rubber."

"Rubber what?" asked Madeline.

"That's the part I can't remember. Well, that and all the other words that went with it. Really, it wasn't a difficult code to break."

"Well, hey, that's great. That's a start. It must be the *r* word that Uncle was starting to say as he slipped into his coma," said Madeline. "Let's sit down and—"

"Oh, no. No more hypnosis. Gave me terrible nightmares, it did. If I remember anything in a *natural* way, I will phone you. Otherwise, leave me alone," said The Marmot, and he jumped into his hole. They could hear doors being slammed and locks being locked.

Madeline, who was having nightmares of her own every night, sympathized. "Well, we have one word, at least."

"*Rubber,*" said Mr. Bunny. "My giant detecting brain is already on the alert."

"Let's give it some thought," said Mrs. Bunny. "In the meantime, I have my hat club meeting this afternoon."

The Bunnys and Madeline got back into the car and started to drive to the hutch.

"How can you go to a hat club meeting with Flo and Mildred still captive?" asked Madeline. "We have to start searching! Let's go search around everything we can think of that has anything to do with rubber."

"*Tch, tch,* that's not methodical," said Mr. Bunny. "Sherlock Holmes had a *method.* That's what I feel we need now. A *method.* My method is to spy on the butler. I shall call it the *butler method.* While Mrs. Bunny is cavorting, you and I will do a little light spying."

"There's no point spying on the *butler,*" said Madeline. "He's got nothing to do with it. We must try to find foxes. Maybe we should even look for factories, in case they have my parents in the rabbit by-product factory."

"Yes, yes, all interesting ideas," said Mr. Bunny, rubbing his chin in a pensive manner. "Let's drive about and look for signs of foxes. And butlers."

"Ignore him," said Mrs. Bunny. "He will never admit he is wrong about the butler."

"We have to get *serious*," said Madeline as they pulled into the Bunnys' driveway. "We can't just flounder around this way."

"Never you mind," said Mr. Bunny. "Wait until you see what I have in the house. It's my greatest invention."

"Another sleepless night?" called Mrs. Bunny as Mr. Bunny ran inside. "Mr. Bunny gets up and invents things when he can't sleep."

"Well, that must be handy," said Madeline.

"Oh yes," said Mrs. Bunny vaguely. "When the basement fills up, I suppose we can sell them for scrap metal."

"Don't they *work*?" asked Madeline.

"Well, he says they do," said Mrs. Bunny.

Mr. Bunny ran back outside. He was carrying a box with a bell on top. "This," he declared proudly, "is a fox finder!"

"Really?" said Madeline. "How does it operate?"

"You see the bell on the top? When the box gets close to

a fox, the bell goes off. I'm telling you, someday I will patent this and make a fortune and Mrs. Bunny will never have to knit again."

"I like knitting," said Mrs. Bunny.

"How does it work exactly?" asked Madeline. "I mean, how does it sense that a fox is about?"

"I don't know," said Mr. Bunny. "Maybe it is magic."

Madeline started to have the uneasy feeling again that she was putting way too much trust in these nice rabbits. On the one hand, it was *so* comforting to have help. On the other hand, to be realistic, they were no help at all. "Well, have you ever tried it before?"

"I've tried it, but of course the bell didn't ring because there were no foxes about. So, in that sense, I think we can say it works fine."

Madeline paused. "Is that all you've got?" she asked finally, but she was interrupted by Mrs. Bunny, who had found an envelope taped to the door, ripped it off, opened and read it.

"Oh, Mr. Bunny!" Mrs. Bunny cried.

"What is it?" asked Mr. Bunny.

"It's a notice."

"I can see that, but a notice from whom?"

"It's not just a notice, it's a summons!"

"Oh no. Not from—"

"Yes! We've been called before . . . *the Bunny Council*."

And then a terrified silence ensued.

MRS. BUNNY WORRIES
THAT PRISON WILL BE BAD
FOR HER COMPLEXION

"Well, I never thought it could happen to us," said Mr. Bunny. "The thing is, the summons might be about so many things. They may be blaming us for the disappearance of the previous owners of the hutch."

"Oh, surely they could not be so unfair," said Mrs. Bunny.

"Can and most likely are!" said Mr. Bunny. "I've read that this is a particularly fierce council, prone to making mistakes and unjust arrests. You can be stripped of your bunny citizenship like *that*!" He snapped his fingers. It made Mrs. Bunny jump. "They could be charging me with driving without a license."

"You said you didn't need one," said Madeline.

"I don't, but they're a capricious bunch," said Mr. Bunny. "Suppose they think it wasn't foxes that got the previous owners but that we killed them for their hutch and car? But the council can't prove it. So they get me on an illegal driving charge and lock me up and throw away the key."

"Mercy, Mr. Bunny!" said Mrs. Bunny. "What a thought!"

"Would you wait for me?"

"For a little while . . . ," said Mrs. Bunny, her eyes wandering. "Perhaps I shall make a few prune cakes and freeze them."

"You mean carrot cakes," said Mr. Bunny, turning to Madeline to explain. "Mrs. Bunny likes prune cakes but never makes them because I don't eat prune."

"He likes prune *plums* but not prunes. Such is the way of the male bunny." Mrs. Bunny rolled her eyes and then continued thoughtfully, "Hmmm. Prune cake or carrot?"

"Not now, Mrs. Bunny," said Mr. Bunny. "This is not the confectionary hour. Try to keep your mind on the facts."

"What facts?" asked Mrs. Bunny. "We have no facts. They ought to at least give us a *hint* as to why we're being called before them."

"That's how they mean to trip you up," said Mr. Bunny. "What's the date on the summons?"

"It says we are to appear before them tomorrow," said Mrs. Bunny, reading it again.

"We don't have *time* for this!" said Madeline, wringing her hands.

"Madeline, dear, this isn't a game. The Bunny Council is a very serious thing indeed," said Mrs. Bunny.

"Finding Flo and Mildred is serious!" said Madeline. "And things keep getting in the way!"

"Don't worry," said Mr. Bunny. "We'll find Flo and Mildred before we get tossed in the clink."

"And then I will have to rescue you too," said Madeline.

"There is no rescuing from a bunny prison," said Mrs. Bunny. "They're very secure."

"Oh dear, oh dear," said Madeline.

"Come on, let's get to work, no sense sitting around worrying," said Mr. Bunny, and they drove Mrs. Bunny to her hat club meeting.

Mrs. Bunny went inside determined to act as if nothing had happened, although the temptation to tell everyone was overwhelming. After all, one of the great things about making friends was all those long and fuzzy sympathetic ears. Still, one never knew how others might react to such tidings, and she was so new to the community. They might not be sympathetic at all. They might *shun* her.

Better not say a word, she thought, or even give hint of such a thing as Mr. Bunny and I going to prison. No, no, no, better keep my bunny lips sealed.

"I have wonderful news," said Mrs. Ruskeebunny as she opened the bunny hat club meeting with a sharp rap of her turnip gavel. "The Bunny Council has approved the making of an extra two hundred bonnets for the march past Comox Elementary. And because Prince Charles's visit is such a singular honor, we are opening up the parade to bunnies from six other counties. All of the parading bunnies will be decked out in our beautifully hand-decorated bonnets."

The hat clubbers clapped their paws together enthusiastically. Bunny applause is never very loud. The fur muffles it. To make up for this, it often goes on for quite a long time. Mrs. Bunny was shaking out her tired clapping paws while thinking she mustn't let anything slip about where she might be in a week. Under no circumstances would she mention prisons.

can we make so many bonnets by then?" asked Mrs. Sneezbunny.

"We will no doubt wear the fur right off our knuckles, but I feel this is a singular honor and we mustn't shrink from it!" said Mrs. Ruskeebunny.

"No indeed," said the rest of the bunnies.

"The council has posted notices everywhere calling for donations of things to decorate the bonnets. This is a true community effort, and so many bunnies started to contribute as soon as they heard donations were needed. That's true bunny nature, and we can all be proud of it. We've had people dropping off their old ribbons and bows and fabric flowers all night, and one very generous anonymous benefactor has donated bolts and bolts of thin rubber to line the bonnets, so we will stop lining the bonnets in plastic and switch to rubber."

"But however can we finish the bonnets with so few meetings before Monday?" asked Mrs. Wigglebunny.

"An excellent question. Indeed, we cannot. Only if we take bonnets home to work on during the week can we hope to finish. Now, I have made up boxes of bonnets and decorations for everyone. I suggest you work on your box of bonnets whenever possible. I myself shall work in front of the television in the evening. And when I chat on the phone with my bunny pals."

"An excellent idea," said Mrs. Hushbunny. "I will do it while waiting for the kettle to boil."

"I will do it during those long empty prison hours," said Mrs. Bunny. "Oh, *curses!*"

"Mrs. Bunny, what *are* you talking about?" asked Mrs. Ruskeebunny.

"Nothing, nothing," said Mrs. Bunny. "My mind wanders."

"Now, I know," said Mrs. Ruskeebunny, "that we ladies won't mind the rather pungent smell of the rubber lining we are putting in the bonnets, but some of us have husbands who may object. Might I ask if any of you have any helpful suggestions for ways to deal with this?"

"A Glade PlugIn," said Mrs. Sneepbunny. "Or several. Put them in every light socket. That should cover the smell."

"My husband would object to a whole house smelling suddenly of Tuberose Surprise," said Mrs. Binglybunny.

"And those Glade PlugIns have a pungent odor of their own," said Mrs. Hopperbunny. "If you plugged them into every light socket the neighbors might complain."

"Or the warden," said Mrs. Bunny. "Or that scary bunny down in cell block D."

"Really, Mrs. Bunny, you make no sense today," said Mrs. Ruskeebunny.

"No, I don't. I really don't. *No* sense. *No* sense at all," said Mrs. Bunny, biting her lips.

"What about candles?" asked Mrs. Hushbunny. "There are some lovely scented ones at the card shoppe."

"Yes, that's fine if they let you have matches in your cell, but they don't," said Mrs. Bunny before she could stop herself.

"Mrs. Bunny, restrain yourself," said Mrs. Ruskeebunny.

"I'm trying," said Mrs. Bunny.

"Why bring the rubber lining home at all? We can decorate the hats at home and then have a special extra meeting just for lining the hats," suggested Mrs. Biliousbunny.

"Ah, now there is a *helpful* suggestion," said Mrs. Ruskeebunny, giving Mrs. Bunny a reproving look.

Mrs. Bunny blushed and blushed.

"We could form an assembly line," said Mrs. Sneepbunny.

"Using the techniques we learned making license plates," said Mrs. Bunny.

"Mrs. Bunny, you are an enigma today," said Mrs. Ruskeebunny.

"What did I say? What did I say?" asked Mrs. Bunny.

"License plates?" said Mrs. Sneepbunny.

"Oh, *curses*! What do I know about license plates? Nothing! Nothing! I don't even drive. What a silly bunny I am. What I meant to say was that an assembly line is an excellent idea!"

"Except that we may not have time for an assembly-line meeting," said Mrs. Snowbunny. "Therefore I suggest we go back to plan A and all buy Glade PlugIns. There are many fine scents that have nothing to do with either tuberose or surprise."

"Excellent!" said the other bunnies, hopping up and down. "Excellent, excellent, excellent!"

And they all hopped home with their boxes of bonnets and decorations, feeling useful and brilliantly intelligent as each remembered the idea as being her own.

Meanwhile, back in the factory basement, the Grand Poobah was pacing back and forth in front of a tired Flo and

Mildred. They had been grilled all night, and for the last two hours without even a single language lesson to relieve the tedium, but still their memories remained a blank.

"Isn't his house by a big tree?" Flo asked Mildred wearily. They had been over this hundreds of times. *Where* exactly was Uncle Runyon?

"Oh, that's no good. There are big trees everywhere on the island. Wasn't there a lake?" asked Mildred.

"I don't think so. There might have been a pond. . . ."

"Wasn't he north of Duncan?"

"YES! YES, he was!"

"Aha!" said the Grand Poobah. "Finally we narrow it down!"

"Or south . . . ," said Flo. "It was one or the other."

"You really should just ask Madeline!" wailed Mildred. "She knows for sure. She probably has the address memorized. That's the type of person she is. I can't believe I gave birth to the type of person who memorizes addresses. My doula never warned me of *that*."

"Ask Madeline? Ask Madeline?" said the Grand Poobah, his face getting progressively redder and his voice louder. "ASK MADELINE? We DID try to ask Madeline. We sent two foxes there in the dead of night to steal her away. And guess what,

Madeline is gone! So we're left with just you. So LET'S START FROM THE BEGINNING! WHERE IS THIS RUNYON'S BLASTED HOUSE?"

"She's gone?" asked Mildred and Flo, looking at each other in alarm. "Where could she be?"

"Well, don't worry, my stupidimentos. She won't be hard to find," said the Grand Poobah. "She is sure to have left a trail. I have my finest foxes scouting for her now. It's only a matter of time. The two of you will be kept alive just until we find her and just until she tells us where this decoder is. Then it's curtains for all of you! You may have lima bean-sized brains, but lima beans, my dears, are very tasty! And guess what? We have been reading your hooman cookbooks and have decided for dinner to have—FINGER FOOD! Guess what the key ingredient is? MWA-HAHA! MWA-HAHA! MWA-DOUBLEHAHAHAHA!"

And he approached them, his grin widening until all they saw were teeth.

▶SOMEONE IS IMPRISONED
AND IT ISN'T THE BUNNYS◀

Mrs. Bunny waited outside for Madeline and Mr. Bunny to pick her up. When they arrived, they seemed tired and discouraged.

"The fox finder found nothing," said Madeline.

"I wouldn't say that," said Mr. Bunny. "We know now where the foxes are *not*. We also know where marmots are not, because we went over to see if The Marmot had remembered anything else, but when we got there he had moved."

"So we Googled his new address and went there," said Madeline.

"But he had moved again by the time we got there," said Mr. Bunny.

"We spent the whole afternoon doing that, and we never did catch up with him," said Madeline.

"And we can't do anything tomorrow morning because we have to go to the Bunny Council," said Mr. Bunny.

"And then what?" said Madeline. "What if they throw you in prison?"

"Nonsense," said Mrs. Bunny stoutly. "Mr. Bunny will never let us get thrown into prison. He'll think of something. He always does. And you must never give up hope, Madeline. I have lived many more years than you, and I can say with certainty that something always turns up. Especially when things look blackest."

"Maybe you should tell the Bunny Council about the foxes' factory. Wouldn't it help if more bunnies were out looking for it? Maybe we need to organize."

"I'm telling you, it's pointless without evidence. We need the translated file card and at least two other pieces of evidence. In fact, the fox SWAT team emergency panic button is right outside the council hall, but there is a terrible fine for pressing it without solid evidence of foxes. And besides, the fox SWAT team will do us no good until we know where the foxes *are*."

"What about the kidnap note?"

"Anyone could have written that. They didn't even sign it 'The Foxes.' They signed it 'The Enemy.' No, be patient, Madeline. We need more."

They rode silently, some of them sulkily, back to the hutch.

When they arrived, there was an envelope stuck to the door. Mrs. Bunny opened it and gasped.

"Great," said Mr. Bunny. "More Bunny Council threats?"

"No," said Mrs. Bunny. "Wait until you read this. This is the break in the case we've been waiting for!"

She passed the note to him and he read, "'So you think you're so smart spying on me, do you? Meet me at the top of the cliff edge, under the oak tree. Signed, your enemy.'"

Madeline squealed. "The foxes! They must have been spying on us while we tried to spy on them!"

"Hmmm," said Mr. Bunny. "It would appear so, but I find it hard to believe that the fox finder didn't sound an alarm. The cliff edge is right before you come to the bunny shopping district. Seems an odd place for foxes. Everyone knows they hate paying retail."

"Let's go right now," said Madeline.

"We can't. It's too late and we have to be up early for the council. I promise we'll go right after the Bunny Council meeting."

"But suppose they throw you in jail?" said Madeline.

"They won't. And whatever you do, Madeline, you are not to go alone. Have you got that?" said Mr. Bunny sternly. "This note is excellent news. It means that those foxes are more scared of us than we are of them, or they would have just kidnapped us today when they had us unawares."

"Why would they be scared of us?" asked Mrs. Bunny. "They weren't scared of Flo and Mildred."

Madeline cleared her throat. "Nobody could be scared of Flo and Mildred. I love them dearly, but they're, well, not exactly fearsome foes. Come on, let's go to the cliff edge now. We can rescue Flo and Mildred and be back in time for the Bunny Council."

"Listen, Madeline, you don't ever want to go after a fox at night. Their night vision is extraordinary, and they're sure to be lying in wait for us. We must hunt them by daylight. Now, Mrs. Bunny and I have a lot on our minds with the council meeting in the morning. You and I have had a busy spy day, and Mrs. Bunny is exhausted from cavorting. We'll go to bed, wake up refreshed and, after the council meeting, charge off to confront this dastardly foe."

"All right," said Madeline. "I guess I could use some rest. Since I can't go to the council meeting with you, I may as well sleep in. Could you not wake me in the morning, please?"

"Of course, dear," said Mrs. Bunny, patting Madeline. She threw Mr. Bunny a look. "You sleep as late as you like."

Mrs. Bunny put Madeline to bed with a glass of warm carrot juice, which was just as delicious as it sounds.

When Mrs. Bunny returned to the hutch, she was surprised to find Mr. Bunny rapidly pacing in front of the fireplace.

"I'm getting worried about Madeline. She's so worked up about those ridiculous parents. She seems to have no faith in our ability to rescue them. She doesn't seem to realize that a bunny always gets his man."

"I think that's a Mountie, dear," said Mrs. Bunny.

"Whatever. I'm sure it applies to rabbits. Anyhow, Madeline is too young for such cares. She should leave it all in our capable detecting paws. And isn't it time to be thinking about her graduation ceremony? It's in two more days. I have an idea, Mrs. Bunny. Instead of you going by bus with the other hat clubbers, why don't I drive you and Madeline up? Then, after the parade, we can go inside and clap our little paws off for Madeline."

"Oh, oh, Mr. Bunny! That is a brilliant plan! Except I think I will even skip the parade. I don't want to risk missing Madeline's big moment."

"Wait a second, what about the white shoes?"

"Let me worry about that. Oh, look, Madeline finally turned out her light. Thank goodness, she is getting some sleep. Let's go up and do the same."

But Mrs. Bunny was wrong. Madeline had closed her light. But she had not gone to sleep.

Madeline crept softly along the ground. The giant moon had waned since Luminara but still glowed behind the clouds, and there was enough starlight to see the way to the edge of town.

"I like the dark. I like the dark," she chanted. "I liked being alone in the dark woods on Hornby."

But this was not the Luminara-lit woods of Hornby, and the errand she was going on was not a carefree one. Instead, she was going over strange countryside to meet with kidnapping murderous carnivorous foxes. This was not a friendly welcoming darkness; it hid things. Leaves fluttered and twigs crunched. Suddenly she regretted going out alone. But she couldn't wait for Mr. and Mrs. Bunny forever. They had their council meeting and might even be in prison tomorrow. And she couldn't wait for her uncle to come out of the coma. Even if he was willing to help her, there was no longer a file card for him to decode. Who knew how much of it he had managed to decode before his coma? The only word they seemed to have was *rubber,* and that was getting them nowhere. No, Flo and Mildred had one person they could count on right now, and that was she. As usual, she alone must save the day.

As Madeline approached the cliff, she spied sawdust arrows on the ground. Clever, she thought. The foxes can easily brush them away afterward, leaving no trace. She moved from arrow to arrow until she came to the oak tree. Now what? she wondered, reading the note again. It didn't say. So she followed the last arrow.

Would the foxes be there under the oak or in the oak, waiting for her all this time? The thought that perhaps they could see her and she couldn't see them chilled her. She turned for a second. Maybe she should come another time. There could be an awful lot of teeth to contend with. Suppose they ate her first and asked questions later? But no, she could not delay.

Madeline walked to the end of the last arrow and started to say, "No guts, no glory," but it came out, "No guts, no glooooooooooooory!" for what looked like firm earth instead gave way and she dropped down, down, down, down, down into darkness.

Madeline dropped a long time before she finally landed in some kind of huge cloth bag. It immediately closed around the top of her head.

Oh no, she thought, I'm trapped.

It was just as total panic ensued that she heard a sound at the top of the hole. A sound oddly like millions of leaves being scuttled about by millions of feet! Fox feet! A voice boomed down into the hole, "HA! At last you are mine! Say your prayers, I've got you now!"

As scared as she was, Madeline felt that there was

something somehow wrong with these words. They were so theatrical. But she'd never spoken to foxes before. Perhaps they had sophisticated thespian societies. Before she had time to think about this, she felt a sharp jerk and the bag was slowly drawn upward.

Now she felt herself being hefted onto the backs of many foxes and carried along. It was not uncomfortable. It was a soft furry bed, but she supposed such comfort would not last long.

Eventually there was the sound of a door opening and she thumped down on a hard cement floor.

"Is anyone there?" asked Madeline in a scared little voice.

"You're mine now!" said the voice.

"I wish you'd stop saying that," said Madeline, rallying. "It's a silly thing to say!"

"Is not. It's scary," said the voice.

There was something about the whiny tone that reminded Madeline of someone, but she couldn't think who.

"Anyhow," the voice went on, "I guess this will teach you to spy on *me*!"

Did the foxes think she and Mr. Bunny had been spying on them? They had been trying to, but they hadn't caught sight of the foxes once. It was she and Mr. Bunny who had been spied on, apparently. She tried to remember if they had glimpsed any sign of foxes, but she didn't think they had. Oh, they really were formidable foes, to stay so well hidden. Anyway, the thing now was to figure a way out. Well, first things first, Madeline thought, and began to try to scratch open a hole in the bag.

Madeline frantically worked at the cotton with her fingers. She was about to try her teeth when she heard the loud clang of a door opening and a whooshing noise as cold air poured into the room. There was the sound of scurrying and then the door clanged shut again.

"Hello?" called Madeline. "Has everyone left? Hello?"

She felt certain there were still foxes in the room. She could smell their slightly musty fur. And then she smelled something else. She couldn't place it at first. Wait, it was garlic!

"Are we on a garlic farm?" she asked.

"Wouldn't you like to know?" came the voice.

"Who are you?" she asked.

"Wouldn't you like to know that too?"

"Where are Flo and Mildred? Are they okay?"

"Who are Flo and Mildred?" taunted the voice once more

before the room grew silent, leaving Madeline alone in the dark. She began to cry.

She had always been so self-sufficient. And that had been fine with her. She took pride in it. Didn't Flo and Mildred like to say she was more of an adult than they were? Didn't she solve their problems for them? She was very good at it. But she didn't want to anymore. She had gotten used to the Bunnys' company. To Mrs. Bunny's soothing cups of tea and Mr. Bunny's complete confidence in every situation. She liked knowing she could rely on them. And she missed her bunny pals! But they'd never find her here. Because of her great self-sufficiency, no one would ever know what happened to her. And the Bunnys themselves might be tossed into prison the next morning and not understand why she never visited them with carrot cakes or tried to plan a daring prison break. They would think she didn't care! Oh, the poor, poor Bunnys! And poor, poor me! Madeline thought. She soaked her bag with tears until she fell asleep.

⊨THE BUNNY COUNCIL⊨

Mr. Bunny slept so badly that he got up at the crack of dawn, put on his overalls and went out to hammer a few shingles onto Madeline's roof. He found hammering always calmed him down.

He lost complete track of time, and before he knew it, Mrs. Bunny was standing in front of the Smart car and calling, "Mr. Bunny, stop that, you'll wake Madeline. And shake a paw, it's time to leave!"

"I thought she was already up," said Mr. Bunny, climbing down his ladder.

"No, no, don't you remember, she asked me not to wake

her this morning. She's exhausted—poor, tired little thing. A morning in bed will do her good. Now hurry!"

She must be able to sleep through anything, thought Mr. Bunny, who had been pounding on her roof for the last hour. "I'll be there in a second. I have to change," he called.

"Are you kidding? We'll be late! Just wear your overalls."

"Overalls?" said Mr. Bunny, coming over to the car. "I can't go wearing my overalls. What will they think? It doesn't show the proper respect. They might arrest me for that alone."

"Nonsense. They'll see me in my lovely black dress and best high heels and they will forget to arrest you because they will be consumed with the question of why such an elegant bunny would marry a zshlob like you."

"I do not like that word, Mrs. Bunny," said Mr. Bunny.

"Come along, let's not talk anymore. We're both nervous and we're sure to quarrel," said Mrs. Bunny.

So they rode in nervous silence all the way to the council hall.

There they found other bunnies waiting outside the courtroom with pale, strained faces.

"See!" said Mr. Bunny. "They're all accessorizing their pale, strained faces with suits."

"Hush," said Mrs. Bunny. Now she was *very* nervous. Suppose they both went to prison? How could they take proper care of Madeline? She wondered how long a little girl could live on prune cakes. She had baked and frozen a dozen. Then she realized Madeline couldn't even get into the hutch to find them. Well, they would simply have to win their case, whatever it was.

The council was running late, as luck would have it, so the Bunnys had an even longer chance to fidget. Mrs. Bunny got a run in her stocking by nervously clawing at it.

"Darn it," she said.

"Shhh," said Mr. Bunny. "You never know what they will think is objectionable language. They may arrest you for that alone and throw you in the clink. Some part of me rather thinks it would serve you right."

Some part of me rather thinks the laugh will be on you when you get home, open the freezer and find nothing to eat but prune cakes, thought Mrs. Bunny. She smiled. Mr. Bunny, seeing her smiling face, thought she had really lost her bunny mind this time. Of course, neither one of them meant these things at all. They were bunny pals forever, through thick and thin.

"Listen, seriously, Mrs. Bunny, this is important. In the courtroom, *never* volunteer information. Got that? Keep the bunny trap shut. In these situations, answer politely and to the point, but *never* volunteer *anything*."

"Okay, okay," muttered Mrs. Bunny, twisting her hand-kerchief. She hated it when Mr. Bunny was emphatic. It made her twice as nervous. It stirred her all up.

Finally the door opened and the Bunnys were called in.

They stood in the dock, looking up at the council, who all sat on very high stools behind a very high table up on a very high stage and stared down at them with great dislike.

And they've never even met us, thought Mrs. Bunny perturbedly.

"So, is your name Mrs. Bunny?" asked the head council-bunny, looking at her sternly.

"Yes," squeaked Mrs. Bunny.

"And are you married to that zshlob in the overalls?"

"I dislike that word," said Mr. Bunny.

"Yes, I am married to the, uh, gentleman in the overalls," said Mrs. Bunny. "But I'd like to add that he was working feverishly hard right up until the time we left and didn't have time to change. He owns a very nice suit too. With cuffs."

"Stop volunteering information," muttered Mr. Bunny out of the side of his mouth.

"Really?" said the head councilbunny acidly. "I hope this putative suit of his is long enough to cover his *PURPLE PLAT-FORM SHOES*!"

There was a stunned silence. However had the council found out about Mr. Bunny's disco shoes?

"Those are my driving shoes," said Mr. Bunny with dignity.

"Well, they are unbecoming to a bunny," said the head councilbunny. "But that is the least of your worries and not why you have been called here. It has been brought to our attention that you have been consorting *WITH MARMOTS*!"

"Curses!" said Mr. Bunny, sotto voce, to Mrs. Bunny. "Someone squealed."

"Wh-wh-what makes you think we consort with marmots?" stuttered Mrs. Bunny.

"Someone at The Olde Spaghetti Factory reported it to us," said the head councilbunny.

"But how did *he* know? The Marmot was in disguise!" said Mrs. Bunny.

"AHA! That is the confession and confirmation we were

looking for. Thank you very much, Mrs. Bunny," said a councilbunny, making a note.

"I told you, *never* volunteer information," whispered Mr. Bunny.

"Silence! That alone would not have been enough to have you thrown in the big pit of snakes," said the head councilbunny.

"You have a big pit of snakes?" interrupted Mrs. Bunny, beginning to shake violently.

"No, I have just always wanted to say that," said the head councilbunny.

"You stop that right now," said Mr. Bunny, shaking his fist. "You're *scaring* Mrs. Bunny."

The council yawned and ignored him.

"But the truly actionable thing you have done is that you have been seen in the company of a HUMAN! A girl human! And you have not even tried to disguise this fact. Not only that, you brought said human to a bunny eating establishment, which goes absolutely against the charter of bunny laws, section six, subcode twelve twenty-three."

"Who says?" said Mr. Bunny.

"A certain bunny waiter."

"I told you to leave a bigger tip," whispered Mrs. Bunny.

"This, in combination with your marmot consorting, has put both of you in a most tenable postion," said the head councilbunny. "Most tenable."

"Perhaps you do not know the meaning of *tenable?*" suggested Mr. Bunny.

"Shhh," said Mrs. Bunny, pinching Mr. Bunny. "Don't make him mad."

"I'll tell you what we have to say," said Mr. Bunny, stepping out of the dock and pacing like a lawyer in the courtroom. "I'll tell you what we have to say. We say, HA!"

"Ha?" asked the head councilbunny.

"You heard me. Ha! Consorting with marmots, I will give you. Or rather, *a* marmot. But let me point out, we all consort with marmots when we need to *decode messages*! Therefore, we are well within our rights and there will be no pit of snakes for us! Ha!"

"True, true," murmured all the councilbunnies.

"Also, we don't have a pit of snakes," whispered one of them.

"True, indeed," Mr. Bunny went on, picking up the pace of his pacing. "No, you can have no objections to *that*. We don't like marmots, but we use them. Am I correct?"

"Nevertheless," said the head councilbunny, "we may *use* marmots, but we don't take them to The Olde Spaghetti Factory. And as for humans, we never, ever befriend them. The waiter reported that the little girl was your *friend*."

"The waiter was wrong. That little girl is *not* our friend," said Mr. Bunny.

"Oh, really?" said the head councilbunny acidly. "She just happened to follow you into The Olde Spaghetti Factory, sit next to you and let you pay for her spaghetti?"

"She is not our friend because she is . . ." And here Mr. Bunny paused for dramatic effect. He paused so long that several councilbunnies went out for coffee. One had time to order a short decaf double shot no whip mocha iced frappuccino to go. Mr. Bunny paused so long that when the councilbunny's coffee came, he had time to change his mind to a venti semi-skim soy no sugar caramel macchiato with no whip but double caramel and a reduced-fat skinny poppy seed and lemon muffin, hot, no butter. When the councilbunnies got back, Mr.

Bunny was almost done pausing. They sipped their coffee and turned their attention back to him.

"OUR PET!" Mr. Bunny finished.

"Your pet? The little girl is a pet?" said the head councilbunny. "A likely story."

"I think if you will read your bunny charter of rights you will find, section sixty-two, subsection nine thirty-four, that, and I quote, 'Bunnies have the inalienable right to have for their pet any animal they choose so long as they build it suitable housing.'"

"AHA!" said the head councilbunny.

"And as you can see, I am wearing my overalls because I was working on the said pet hutch right up until council time! HA! HAHAHAHA, HAHA!" said Mr. Bunny triumphantly.

"Curses! The dreaded loophole!" the councilbunnies muttered to each other.

"And if any of you should care to follow us home, you will find this fantastic pet hutch!" said Mr. Bunny, wildly waving around his arms in an excited and exaggerated fashion.

"I don't think," said the headcouncilbunny, "that any of us care to, as you so unlawyerlikely put it, 'follow you home.' We will send an official building inspector to check on this story.

I suggest there had better be a pet house for this human when the inspector arrives. That's all I have to say. NEXT!"

"I haven't made my closing arguments!" protested Mr. Bunny, still waving his arms around. He found it very aerating.

"NEXT!" said the head councilbunny again, and in were led a terrified pair of suit-wearing bunnies.

"Stand firm," said Mr. Bunny, gripping the upper arm of one of the accused bunnies. "Don't let them cheat you out of a closing argument! And when you pause for dramatic effect, that's a good time to put in your coffee order."

"And there is no pit of snakes!" whispered Mrs. Bunny.

Then, having done all they could, they hopped back to the car.

Mr. and Mrs. Bunny drove the first few miles home in exhausted silence. Finally, Mrs. Bunny said, "Brilliant, Mr. Bunny. I never thought of keeping Madeline on as our pet."

"I can't wait to tell her. We can keep her always," said Mr. Bunny.

Mrs. Bunny frowned. "But what about her parents?"

"The ones who won't come to her parent-teacher conferences? To heck with them," said Mr. Bunny fiercely. "I'll tell you another thing, I'm not going back to The Olde Spaghetti Factory. Now that I know they have *tattling* waiters."

"You ought to tip more," said Mrs. Bunny.

"The problem isn't with the tipping," said Mr. Bunny. "It's the employers' job to pay their waiters a decent wage. If they did this, then the waiters would not have to rely on tips. I do not like to feel obligated to pay the wages of a restaurant's employees. . . ."

And on and on and on Mr. Bunny went with this well-worn argument. Mrs. Bunny had heard it a million times before and could not imagine what had possessed her to bring it up again. Mr. Bunny was still talking about it as they drove home. And as he parked and got out and as Mrs. Bunny collected the mail and put it in the house. She tried stuffing his mouth full of circulars, but she could still hear him talking. Then she tried socks. But he was still making sounds. She was considering duct tape, but she wasn't fast enough.

"Let's give Madeline the good news," she said, giving up and going into Madeline's hutch while Mr. Bunny spit socks out over the back lawn. His projectile range was excellent.

"Madeline!" they called out cheerily.

But Madeline was gone.

"Where could she be?" asked Mrs. Bunny.

"Maybe she got hungry and went to pick some lettuces," said Mr. Bunny, so they hopped around the garden, but Madeline was nowhere to be found. Hmm, he thought, the lettuces were looking a little dry. Should he tell Mrs. Bunny a sad story?

"Oh, Mr. Bunny, we should have taken her with us. I felt so from the start," said Mrs. Bunny, punching him on the arm.

"Ouch! Get ahold of yourself, Mrs. Bunny. If you felt so, you never said so."

"Oh, Mr. Bunny," wailed Mrs. Bunny. "You don't suppose she was foolish enough to go to the cliff edge alone? We told her to wait for us."

"I'm afraid that is what she did do," said Mr. Bunny grimly. "Hurry!"

They leapt into the car and drove to the cliff edge. There they leapt out to look for clues. They found signs of markings that had been carefully smudged out.

"What was it, do you think?" asked Mrs. Bunny as Mr. Bunny sifted through the sawdust debris. "A message?"

"No," said Mr. Bunny. "A line, and see, the remnant of another. Mrs. Bunny, I think it's a trail! Let's follow the debris."

Mr. and Mrs. Bunny hopped along these remnants until they came to the oak tree. There seemed to have been one last smudge. Mrs. Bunny hopped excitedly in that direction until Mr. Bunny's hand grabbed her and pulled her back. "Stop!" he cried, and pointed down one hop ahead of where Mrs. Bunny stood.

Mrs. Bunny turned pale. "The snake pit! There *was* one after all," she whispered in awe, and promptly fainted.

"For heaven's sake," said Mr. Bunny, yanking Mrs. Bunny to her feet. "Wake up!"

"Oh, Mr. Bunny," squealed Mrs. Bunny, having been roused by Mr. Bunny, who in his excitement might have bitten her just a little. "They've got Madeline! Let's jump in after her! We can stomp those snakes with our floppy feet!"

Mr. Bunny put a restraining paw on Mrs. Bunny. "Wait, let's not go off half-cocked, Mrs. Bunny, with more enthusiasm than brains. Let us certainly not start jumping into holes. We are not detectives for nothing. Let's us sit here for a minute and think."

The Bunnys sat. If there was ever a time for the brains under those fuzzy ears and fetching fedoras, it was now.

Mr. Bunny suddenly stood up.

"Mrs. Bunny," he said, "I have an idea."

Madeline was awoken by someone opening the bag she lay curled tightly inside.

"It's morning. We are going to take you out of this bag and blindfold you and lead you to the bathroom," said a whiny voice. "But if you resist or give us trouble, it's back in the bag for you. Got it?"

"Oh, for heaven's sake," said Madeline. She didn't know why the tone of the speaker exasperated her so much. She felt she herself could be a scarier villain than this apparent guard fox, but nevertheless she thought it best to cooperate.

When she returned from the bathroom and the blindfold was removed, she found herself in pitch-darkness. Metal banged on metal, and she heard loud stomping feet. There was a pungent smell of garlic. From somewhere in the room she heard the sound of many mouths chewing.

Occasionally a voice would call out. Sometimes the voice was high. Sometimes it was low. Sometimes it had a Spanish accent. Sometimes a French accent. Always it said the same thing: "Now you are mine!" It was maddening and monotonous and Madeline wished she knew what it meant.

Then, just as Madeline thought she was going to go crazy if she heard "Now you are mine!" one more time, the voices switched to "Beware, the boss is coming!"

Now, this did worry Madeline. Maybe this whiny-voiced fox wasn't much threat, but the boss might be a different story. It was time to make a move. She crept slowly away from the voices until she found a wall. Then, feeling her way along the wall, she tiptoed sideways, hoping to find a door. Inch by inch she moved, worrying that the foxes would notice what she was doing, but they seemed busy nattering in different accents. At last her hands came upon a doorknob. She sighed in relief. She turned it, but to no avail. She was locked in. She almost wept in frustration, when suddenly she remembered the tae kwon do that KatyD had taught her. She rehearsed the sideways kick in her mind. The boss fox, when he entered, would have a surprise waiting for him!

There Madeline stood, poised and ready as the moments ticked on. Finally, just as she was about to sit down again, the door swung open. She leapt sideways, kicked where she thought the boss's collarbone should be and met air. She fell over and the door swung the rest of the way open. Any second she expected sharp teeth, but what the light revealed was the last thing she expected.

⊁A CLUE!⊁

There stood Mr. Bunny, holding The Marmot by the scruff of his neck in one paw and another marmot in the other paw. Both marmots were munching garlic bread and looking completely unfazed, even when Mr. Bunny heaved them across the room onto a pile of other marmots and flicked the lights on.

"MR. AND MRS. BUNNY!" cried Madeline when she could find her voice.

"Yes, for so we are called!" proclaimed Mr. Bunny, and then the three of them fell upon each other in furry joy.

When everyone had calmed down, Madeline stared at the pile of garlic-bread-munching marmots in the corner in a state

of disbelief. "I've been in here with marmots all this time? But what about the accents? The scary voices?"

"Digital voice-changing box. Very deluxe item as seen on TV," said The Marmot.

"Oh, I've seen commercials for that! Does it really work?" asked Mrs. Bunny, forgetting herself and hopping over to their corner to examine it.

"Sure it does, sure it does, it's seen on *TV*! You just speak into the microphone here and it changes your voice," said The Marmot through a mouthful of garlic bread.

"How clever!" said Mrs. Bunny. "How much was it?"

"Twelve ninety-nine. And if you order now you get the Instaburp absolutely free! Of course, it comes to a hundred dollars by the time you add the shipping and handling."

"Yes, that's how they always get you, the shipping and handling," said Mrs. Bunny, nodding sagely and then remembering herself. "Still, it serves you right, you naughty naughty marmot! I wish they'd charged you DOUBLE!"

"Well, that's a bit harsh," said The Marmot, grabbing a piece of bread from another marmot, which started a free-for-all among them as they scrabbled for the last bits. There were crumbs everywhere.

"So *you're* the enemy?" asked Madeline. She was still baffled. "But I thought foxes took Flo and Mildred!"

For a second the room froze and fur quivered. Marmots were no fonder of foxes than bunnies were. Then they shrugged it off. It was always out of sight, out of mind with marmots.

"Yes, I'm the enemy, like the note said," said The Marmot. "And why wouldn't I be your enemy? First Mr. Bunny gives me a vicious pinch, then you hypnotize me and probably make me do things like sing like Elvis. *I'll* never know. *I* was hypnotized!"

"Oh, don't be silly," said Madeline.

"And then my neighbors tell me that you were following me from new hole to new hole, spying on me. Well, I guess I showed you! I guess I turned the tables on you! HA! You won't be calling me stupid marmot anymore."

"I think I can assure you, I will always call you stupid marmot," said Mr. Bunny.

"But how did you find me?" asked Madeline to Mr. and Mrs. Bunny.

"AND," The Marmot interrupted, "I got hundreds of friends to help me capture you and carry you here. That's a marmot community for you. Won't find that kind of community spirit with rabbits."

"Hundreds?" said Mr. Bunny skeptically.

"Well, sixteen," said The Marmot, starting in on another piece of garlic bread.

"Oh, shut up, you ridiculous Marmot," said Mr. Bunny, who had had enough. "Mrs. Bunny and I got to the pit, and when we saw all the branches about, we realized that they had covered it and used it to trap you, Madeline. We were looking for foxes, of course, but what we found was an unusually high concentration of marmot fur. Marmots are always shedding."

"Aren't," said The Marmot.

"We knew that if The Marmot was hiding you, it would have to be somewhere you could fit, which would rule out their holes."

"We thought you might still be down in the deep snake-pitty hole," said Mrs. Bunny. "I was all set to leap down and stomp those snakes with my floppy feet when Mr. Bunny had an *idea*!"

"Yes," said Mr. Bunny. "I *looked* in the hole. It was quite deep but not so deep you could not see to the bottom. There was no Madeline to be seen. And no snakes either." He paused a second and gave Mrs. Bunny a look.

"There very well might have been," said Mrs. Bunny primly.

Mr. Bunny gave her another look as if to suggest that it was a great trial to be on constant idiot patrol and then went on. "Then I thought, where would The Marmot go? What is The Marmot's favorite place on earth?"

"The Olde Spaghetti Factory," said Madeline.

"Precisely. We circled the building. They happened to be delivering cans of sauce as we arrived. They were sending cartons down this big chute, and we figured that was how The Marmot got you in, so we slid down the chute and hopped about until we found the room where they store the garlic bread. There sat The Marmot and a couple of pals chewing their way through a carton of it. It was the work of a moment to persuade them to show us where they had hidden you."

"Poor dear," said Mrs. Bunny. "You must have been so frightened. Don't you ever go off on your own like that again."

"Well, anyhow, you're safe now," said Mr. Bunny, leading Madeline toward the door. "They've all eaten so much garlic bread they couldn't defend their fortress of carbohydrates even if they wanted to."

"But where are Flo and Mildred?"

"Who's that? Who's that?" asked The Marmot.

Madeline's heart sank. If the note to meet the enemy by the cliff edge had nothing to do with Flo and Mildred, she was no closer to finding them than she'd ever been, and yet more time had been wasted.

"I suggest we all go home. And YOU!" said Mr. Bunny, turning to The Marmot and shaking his fist. "What do you have to say about *that*?"

"I was only kidding anyway," said The Marmot, who had finished his garlic bread and was now embroiled in a fight over which button to push next on the voice-disguising box and didn't even notice when the Bunnys and Madeline left.

When they got back to the hutch, it was dark. Madeline had had very little sleep the night before, and despite the fact that she wanted to set right out again to find Flo and Mildred, Mrs. Bunny made her go to bed.

"Listen, dear," said Mrs. Bunny gently, tucking her in, "tomorrow is another day. Get some sleep. As long as the foxes don't know where your uncle lives, your parents should still be safe."

Madeline wanted to stay awake, but her eyes kept drooping. She was fast asleep before Mrs. Bunny could turn off the light.

Mrs. Bunny tiptoed out. Mr. Bunny was waiting for her.

"It does not look good for Flo and Mildred," he whispered.

"At least as long as Madeline is with us, *she* will be safe," Mrs. Bunny whispered back.

"Tomorrow is her graduation," said Mr. Bunny.

"I very much fear she will want to skip it in order to look for her parents," said Mrs. Bunny.

"Dear, dear," said Mr. Bunny. "Let's go inside and give our brains a rest. There must be a clue we have somehow missed. In books there always is. I feel sure that if we turn our attention to soothing pursuits, this clue will suddenly leap out at us!"

"We still have the word *rubber*," Mrs. Bunny reminded him.

"Ah!" said Mr. Bunny.

Mr. and Mrs. Bunny went inside and settled in front of the fire. Mr. Bunny picked up his article on things that explode, and Mrs. Bunny began lining a bonnet with rubber. She had a box of them she had brought home from the meeting and she hadn't had time to get to any of them yet.

"Oh my goodness, I am tired," she said. "Between the bonnet trimming and the detecting, I am quite done in, and I need to finish these before bed. I hope Mrs. Treaclebunny doesn't show up at our door tonight. I would like to put on my jammies, have a quiet supper and go to bed without speaking to any other bunnies."

"Excepting myself," said Mr. Bunny.

"Always excepting yourself."

"Ah, well, I have been thinking about that, Mrs. Bunny, and here is my idea. We put a pile of everything that Mrs. Treaclebunny could possibly ever want to borrow outside our door along with a plate of dinner and then we post a sign saying 'Help yourself.' She need never ring the bell and we can have a peaceful uninterrupted evening. And maybe *then* I can solve the rubber clue."

"Mr. Bunny, sometimes I think you are a genius!" said Mrs. Bunny, clasping her paws over her heart.

"When do you not think I'm a genius?" asked Mr. Bunny in dismay.

And that is what they did. They piled lawn mowers, Kleenex, left-handed corkscrews, saltines, Ping-Pong balls, snow cones, DVDs, soy hot dogs, small bars of shell-shaped guest soaps and many more things outside the door in one glorious pile. Mrs Bunny put a foil-wrapped paper plate of carrot and onion loaf next to it. She worried that it wouldn't stay warm, but Mr. Bunny suggested that Mrs. Treaclebunny probably had a microwave like everyone else. Mrs. Bunny said but what if she didn't and worried and worried until finally she wrote a little Post-it that said, *Place in 325 degree oven for half an hour. A tablespoon of water in the pan will keep it moist.*

Then they settled back in their chairs and Mr. Bunny continued reading aloud:

"'Many new exploding things can be found in common household materials, although some, such as the following, are for industrial, not common household exploding: industrial plastics, industrial fiberglasses, industrial laminates . . .'"

"They certainly like the word *industrial*," said Mrs. Bunny.

"How else would you describe something from industry?"

"I don't know, but I can't help thinking they could find a less tiresome word."

"'. . . And industrial rubber.'" And here Mr. Bunny stopped. He put the magazine down. Mrs. Bunny looked up. He wasn't moving. She stopped sewing and watched him interestedly to see if he was perhaps going to have a fit of some kind. His mouth was a perfect O.

Finally, when it became clear that he wasn't going to do

anything conclusively sensational, she sighed disappointedly and said, "Mr. Bunny, spit it out."

"I had a thought, but now it's gone. But never mind, because, oh, my ears and whiskers, what is that horrible smell exuding from your direction? Have you begun to rot, Mrs. Bunny?"

"Oh no, Mr. Bunny, I'm afraid it's just the rubber lining I've brought home to put in these bonnets. You see, we were left with bolts of it by some anonymous donor. It was a generous if smelly gesture. It will keep everyone's head dry if it rains. I wouldn't bother with the linings myself, but our hat club president insists."

"Well, it's going to be a smelly parade, is all I can say. I hope the prince brought nose plugs."

"Speaking of which, could you drive to the hat shoppe in the morning while I make breakfast and let Mrs. Ruskeebunny know that I will not be with them on one of the Greyhound buses? Could you take her the finished bonnets as well? Tell her we will meet the other bunnies there if we are able to find Flo and Mildred first."

"Of course. In the meantime, let's go to bed. I'm sure the Case of the Word *Rubber* will solve itself in my dreams."

"In your dreams, is right," said Mrs. Bunny.

"Mrs. Bunny, if I did not know you better, I would think you were being unkind."

"Nonsense, Mr. Bunny, I'm so excited that you're about to crack the case that I can hardly concentrate."

"You can hardly concentrate anyway, Mrs. Bunny. Now let's go to bed."

But once in bed, Mr. Bunny was kept awake by Mrs. Bunny's twitching feet.

"What in the world is the matter with you?" asked Mr. Bunny.

"I am worried about Mrs. Treaclebunny. She has not knocked on the door, and I am afraid she is sitting all alone in her hutch, unsuppered, unlended and unloved. She probably never has any real meals. Maybe she doesn't even have a stove, just a few crackers by the bed."

"She has an *ocean view,*" said Mr. Bunny, and promptly fell asleep.

►PUSHING THE PANIC BUTTON◄

Mr. Bunny hopped out the door early.

"Where is he going?" asked Madeline.

"Um, he needs a furcut," said Mrs. Bunny. "In the midst of detecting and other, um, important things, it is important to remember to stay well groomed."

The Bunnys had agreed not to tell Madeline that Mrs. Bunny might miss her parade in order to find Flo and Mildred. Madeline had obviously forgotten that today was the graduation and the parade of bonnets in front of Prince Charles. The Bunnys felt it better not to mention that either.

"Let's make pancakes outside on the barbecue!" said Mrs. Bunny, trying to distract her.

"But won't they fall through the grill?" asked Madeline.

"That's just what makes it so challenging!" said Mrs. Bunny, and went inside to whip up some batter.

Mr. Bunny sped down the road. He didn't even bother to find parking but abandoned the car on Main Street and ran to the hat shoppe. He couldn't wait to drop off the bonnets and go back to find Flo and Mildred. Today was sure to be the day, and afterward they could watch Madeline win her awards!

The shoppe was locked, and while he waited for Mrs. Ruskeebunny to come and open it, he peered in the window. All those rubber-lined bonnets. Something that had been niggling at the back of his brain suddenly came to the forefront. Rubber! The word from the file card that The Marmot remembered. *Exploding* rubber! The article! Little bunny heads exploding all over the place. Could this be the work of foxes? Perhaps the very foxes who had kidnapped Flo and Mildred?

There was no time to puzzle this out. Action was called for! Mrs. Bunny never put two and two together, but she did not have his big detecting brain. Her own was the size of a kidney bean. Wasn't this smelly rubber they were lining the bonnets with *industrial*? The same kind of rubber that *The Scientific Bunny* claimed exploded? Someone was going to have to save all these bunnies from unsuspected carnage. It was *HE*! No mere detective he, but *SUPER*bunny! How he wished he had time to put on a cape. But there was not a moment to lose!

Mr. Bunny found a rock and broke the glass in the front door, reached in and unlocked it from the inside. Once inside, he began ripping bonnets to pieces as quickly as he could. Sequins and ribbons flew everywhere. It was the only way! Those lovely lady bunnies wouldn't become furry fireworks. Not on his watch!

Using scissors and his teeth and claws, he destroyed nearly every bonnet in the shoppe. It was necessary work at first, and then he discovered he rather liked it. Perhaps someday he would teach a course in it.

He was trying to rip them in time to a little salsa ditty he had running in his head when the door opened and Mrs.

Ruskeebunny entered. She gave an ear-piercing scream and shouted, "What are you doing? What are you doing!"

"Ummm." Mr. Bunny came to with a start and surveyed the mess about the shoppe. Well, maybe it wasn't such a good sport after all. It would probably never catch on like, say, tennis. "I think I may have gotten a little carried away. A little swept up in the moment. Anyhow, unimportant, what I came to tell you was that I would be driving Mrs. Bunny up to the parade if we come at all, so don't hold the bus for her."

Mrs. Ruskeebunny looked at the torn-apart bonnets. "AAAAAA!" she screamed again.

It was at that exciting moment that Mr. Bunny, who was trying to figure out how to explain the complicated plot twists to Mrs. Ruskeebunny, froze completely; he wasn't quite sure he understood them himself—file cards and foxes and issues of *The Scientific Bunny* were jumbled in his head, not to mention the vision of himself standing on a podium receiving a large hero's medal from some hazy but important figure. His mouth worked, but no sounds came out.

He noticed that Mrs. Ruskeebunny was herself wearing a wholly intact rubber-lined bonnet. It occurred to him that if the rubber was the exploding type, it had had plenty of opportunity to do so. They were probably safe with these bonnets after all. And yet, oddly, his fingers still itched to rip Mrs. Ruskeebunny's bonnet off her head and stomp on it. Perhaps he would need to join a support group.

"Um, nice bonnet," he said, pointing to it. "Is it new?"

Mrs. Ruskeebunny just glared. Her expression was quite fierce. Mr. Bunny decided not to explain himself. He was short of time. He would leave the explanations to Mrs. Bunny. She was better at it anyway.

"I may have made, a, um, little mistake," he said, backing toward the door. "But let me ask you this. I know you ladies enjoy making bonnets, but have you ever tried ripping them apart? It's strangely invigorating."

"Little mistake?" Mrs. Ruskeebunny cried, advancing on him. "Look what you did to the parade bonnets! How do you suggest I repair them in time?"

"Krazy Glue?" asked Mr. Bunny, smiling nervously.

Then he decided it was time to go.

Mrs. Bunny was coming out of the hutch with some pan-cake batter when she spied a note on her door. Notes were never good. She was getting sick of notes. She took it down and opened it with trembling fingers.

> Dear inhospitable bunnies,
>
> I have borrowed many things in my time and eaten many other people's suppers but <u>never</u> have I been treated so shabbily. Never has anyone <u>left</u> the food and borrowed items on the porch steps. You needn't worry. I can take a hint.

Since when, thought Mrs. Bunny?

> I shall not darken your door again. And if you put some curry powder in your carrot loaf it would taste less like dog food. I should know; before Mr. Treaclebunny and I bought our rubber factory, we had a dog food factory. We used old carrot loaf. Yours would have been very suitable.
>
> Yours truly,
> Isadora Treaclebunny

"Rubber factory?" said Mrs. Bunny, and hopped like the wind across to Mrs. Treaclebunny's, where she banged on the door.

"Come in, come in," said Mrs. Treaclebunny. "I'm just making myself some decent-tasting carrot loaf. Perhaps you'd like another cooking tip or two. Or a hospitality tip. Or a common decency tip. Or a good manners tip. Or . . ." She went on in this vein, calling out suggestions for tips over her shoulder as she hopped to her kitchen with Mrs. Bunny following.

No kitchen? Crackers by the bed? How Mrs. Bunny had been wrong!

Mrs. Treaclebunny had a kitchen larger than the Bunnys' whole hutch and filled with every appliance known to rabbits. A pasta maker and a KitchenAid mixer sat on the counter. There was a fancy Sub-Zero fridge, a restaurant stove and walls and walls of cabinets. There was a kitchen island with all kinds of built-in devices. There were bowls of fresh exotic fruit everywhere, and loaves of homemade bread, and windows looking out over the ocean.

"Rubber factory?" began Mrs. Bunny, and then something caught her eye. "Where did you get that?" She pointed to the bolts of rubber lining stacked in a corner. "Were you lining bonnets?"

"Oh no, I've been trying to get rid of this stuff for ages. Stinks. My dead-as-a-doornail-husband's company used to make it, and it's been smelling up his factory basement forever. I sold the factory a few weeks ago on Craigslist. It couldn't have been easier until I got the email from the buyers insisting I remove the rolls of rubber from the basement. What a bunch of fussbudgets. I took it home but afterwards had a terrible time getting rid of the stuff. Smells so bad even the dump wouldn't take it. Then I heard the hat shoppe was calling for donations. Donations, I'll give them donations, I said to myself. Yuk, yuk, yuk."

"*You* left the rubber at the hat shoppe? *You're* the anonymous donor?" asked Mrs. Bunny.

"Listen, take a few rolls with you. Can't beat it for wallpaper," said Mrs. Treaclebunny.

"No, thank you," said Mrs. Bunny, a tad icily.

"Line your pet's litter box?"

"Madeline doesn't use a litter box! The idea!"

"I hear it makes excellent soup."

"Oh, now you're just being silly," said Mrs. Bunny.

"It's delicious when sautéed."

"Never mind that, does it explode?" asked Mrs. Bunny. She suddenly remembered the article Mr. Bunny was reading. Mr.

Bunny would never put two and two together like this. His brain was the size of a kidney bean.

"Do you *want* it to?" asked Mrs. Treaclebunny.

"Oh, for heaven's sakes, I take that as a no. Never mind. Listen, you didn't see the name of the new factory, did you?"

"Sure, it's not printed on the outside yet, but inside it says 'Something something rabbit products and by-products.' Oddly, it's written in Fox."

Mrs. Bunny leapt into the air. "You silly bunny!" she shouted. "Didn't you stop to think that you had sold your factory to a bunch of foxes who planned to TURN US INTO BY-PRODUCTS? Wasn't the fact that it was written in Fox a *clue*?"

Mrs. Treaclebunny quivered. "I thought rabbit products meant products made by rabbits. And who the heck knows what by-products are? I did think it was odd that it was written in Fox. But, oh my, so much of life is inexplicable, don't you find? Oh dear."

"Oh, you ridiculous bunny! Did you see a couple of humans tied up in the basement?"

"Like that wouldn't have gotten my attention. What do you take me for?"

"Let's not get into that now. There's no time to lose. We must get Madeline and go to the Bunny Council and press the panic button! I'm sure the foxes have hidden Flo and Mildred at the rubber factory."

Mrs. Treaclebunny had always wanted to push the panic button. "Wahoo! I'll drive," she cried.

"I didn't know you had a car," said Mrs. Bunny.

"A scooter," said Mrs. Treaclebunny.

"Get it and meet me at my hutch!" yelled Mrs. Bunny over her shoulder as she sped off.

"Who are Flo and Mildred?" cried Mrs. Treaclebunny.

"I'll explain later!"

Mrs. Bunny ran home and grabbed Madeline. "I know where the fox factory is! They've remade the old rubber factory. Your parents are sure to be there! Hurry!"

"Oh, Mrs. Bunny, if anyone were to find them, I was sure it would be you!" cried Madeline.

"Well, it wouldn't be Mrs. Treaclebunny, that's for darn tootin'! Now, let's just write a quick note to Mr. Bunny telling him where we have gone. Mrs. Treaclebunny is going to take us on her scooter. There is no time to lose!"

Out the door they flew to the road, where Mrs. Treacle-bunny was waiting. Mrs. Bunny climbed into the scooter basket, and Madeline got on behind Mrs. Treaclebunny, who kept saying, "Who the heck is *this*?"

"We'll explain the whole thing on the way!" yelled Mrs. Bunny over the roar of the scooter. "There's no time to lose."

Madeline lifted her knees high and off they zipped. Mrs. Treaclebunny was an intrepid driver. Mrs. Bunny's paws went right over her eyes. She and Madeline yelled the story to Mrs. Treaclebunny, who was very excited about her part in the rescue. She had visions of herself at a podium receiving a medal from some hazy but important figure.

When they got to the Bunny Council hall, all three of them leapt off the scooter. There was quite a skirmish over who would get to push the button first, but in the end they all pushed it, unwittingly setting off what was known in Bunny Emergency Preparedness as a Three-Push Alarm. Suddenly rabbits began pouring out of the police station, all suited up in hound costumes and donning large hound heads. Two fire trucks roared out of the fire station, their horns blaring the barks and howls of hound dogs. They went racing down the road until they realized they didn't know where they were going, so they turned around and headed back to find whoever had set off the alarm.

"Where are they? Where are they?" called the heroic bunny hound patrol to Mrs. Treaclebunny, Mrs. Bunny and Madeline.

"Follow me!" said Mrs. Treaclebunny, who was intent on leading the rescue.

"Just give us the address, ma'am. We're professionals," said the chief of the SWAT team.

"Turnips to you, mister," said Mrs. Treaclebunny. "This is my case."

"Technically this is my case," said Mrs. Bunny.

"Will someone please just RESCUE MY PARENTS!" wailed Madeline.

"Wait a second," said the chief. "We can't use the emergency teams to rescue a human."

"She's my pet," said Mrs. Bunny.

"And besides," said Madeline, "the foxes are starting a rabbit products and by-products factory."

"What's a by-product?" asked a SWAT team member.

"NEVER MIND WHAT A BY-PRODUCT IS!" yelled

Madeline. "CAN WE JUST GET GOING? THEY'RE AT THE RUBBER FACTORY!"

"TO THE RUBBER FACTORY!" shouted the chief, and off they all started again, hounds howling and barking from the loudspeakers and hound heads securely over bunny ears.

"Hey, you weren't supposed to give the address! This was my rescue operation! I want to be in front," said Mrs. Treaclebunny to Madeline as she zoomed down the road, passing police cars and fire trucks and driving between cars and on the shoulder of the road until finally she was once again leading the way.

"Oh my saints, oh my saints," chanted Mrs. Bunny through gritted teeth. She had her paws over her eyes, but she kept peeking out to find herself between a truck and a speeding car coming from opposite directions. "Mrs. Treaclebunny, nobody should drive like this. Even Mr. Bunny wouldn't drive like this."

Mrs. Treaclebunny gave her a withering glance and gunned it.

Down in the factory basement, the Grand Poobah had been advancing toothily upon Flo and Mildred when a bevy of fox waitresses appeared with trays of finger food that the Grand Poobah had forgotten he had ordered.

"Ah! Tea!" he said. And then, because breeding will tell, he had offered the trays to everyone, including Flo and Mildred, whom he still aspired to teach at least one word of Fox. By now it had become a personal challenge.

They were all having a delightful munch when suddenly there was the sound of dogs howling and barking.

"What's that sound, man?" Flo asked the Grand Poobah.

"Not 'What's that sound,' you idiotoman. I said '*Zamboosi-doey*,' which means 'Have a sandwich.' Now try it again."

"No, I mean the barking," said Flo.

"There is no barking. There are no dogs for miles around. Do you not think we would check before buying a factory? Now try it again, '*Zamboosidoey*.'"

"I hear it, too," said Mildred. "Dogs."

"You wish," said the Grand Poobah.

Just then, Frederick came barreling down the stairs, knocking foxes and their trays of finger food over in his haste. "Poobah! Poobah! HOUNDS! A FOX HUNT!"

"Curses! Frankie Fox, pack up the food in Tupperwares and let's GET OUT OF HERE!" yelled the Grand Poobah. "ME

FIRST!" and he ran up the stairs, followed by all the foxes except Frankie, who was frantically putting sandwiches into containers, until at last he fled as well.

"Now we'll never learn Fox," whined Flo.

But then something even more astonishing happened. Dozens of hounds jumped out from every door and window. And oddly, they were all hopping. Leading the way down the stairs was Madeline!

"FLO!" she shouted. "MILDRED! You're alive!"

"Yeah, but man, like I said, I think I was just on the verge of a breakthrough in Fox. Like ten more minutes and I would have had it, man."

"How did you know we were here?" asked Mildred, glaring at Flo. They had been tied back to back for several days and she had just about had it with him.

"It's a long story," said Madeline, running over to untie her parents, and told them about Uncle Runyon's coma and the Bunnys. "But are you sure you're okay? I've been so worried!"

Then, remembering how worried she had been even a couple of hours previously, Madeline began to cry in relief. And once she started she couldn't stop.

Flo looked at her as if she were from the moon.

"But hey, we are all right, man!" he said. "Like, I don't have to learn Fox. I could study, like, Hindi maybe."

"There, there," said Mildred awkwardly. She could remember Madeline being exasperated plenty of times. She had experience dealing with *that*. But this crying business was brand-new. "No need to worry. As you can see, we're just fine. Although I may have to go on a spiritual retreat very soon to rebalance my chakras."

"Cool," said Flo. "I could, like, totally get into doing that with you."

"No, you couldn't," said Mildred. "Anyhow, good finding, Madeline. As usual, you were very efficient."

"Yeah, man, we had faith in you. We figured you'd probably find us. Or, like, find something else."

"You have faith in me? Find something *else*? What *else*?" said Madeline. "And weren't you just a little worried? Or worried that *I'd* be worried?"

"Mostly I was worried that you *wouldn't* find us. Like, I've got faith in you, but even we didn't know where we were," said Flo. "Or I worried, you know, I would never learn Fox. The Grand Poobah kept losing it. Man, that dude shouldn't be a teacher. He's got, like, a low frustration tolerance."

Oh, I give up, thought Madeline. Then she realized she very nearly hadn't found them and she began a whole new meltdown. She sobbed again, this time with a dripping nose and a lot of snorting, snorking noises. One of the SWAT team members handed her a handkerchief. Another wrapped her in a quilt the bunnies made for victims, having looked at Flo and Mildred and decided Madeline qualified.

"Now what?" asked Flo. "I've never *seen* you like this. You seem, like, stressed."

"OF COURSE I'M STRESSED!" screamed Madeline.

"C'mon, chill out, dude," said Flo, looking at her in alarm and patting her gingerly on the back.

"I think we all need a little lavender essential oil," said Mildred. "We'll check on Runyon and then go home and douse ourselves with it. Maybe Runyon has some. Do you think?"

A SWAT team member finally got the ropes binding Flo and Mildred loose, and after shaking out their limbs, they went over and hugged Madeline.

"I very much doubt Uncle has lavender essential oil," said Madeline dryly, wiping away her tears.

"But, man, it was an *experience.* Talking foxes. They spoke *English!* Way cool."

"Are you starving? Did they feed you?"

"Oh, yes, we had, uh, excellent finger food," said Mildred. "Eggplant-paste sandwiches."

"Yeah, those foxes are all right!" said Flo.

"They are *not*," said the chief with affronted dignity. "Whatever foxes are, they are certainly *not* all right."

"We had crudités and dip and stuffed mushrooms. Too bad they packed it in Tupperwares and took it with them," said Flo.

"Speaking of mushrooms, I'm beginning to feel like one. Can we go outside now?" said Mildred, rubbing her aching arms where they had been tied up.

Outside, Mrs. Bunny and Mrs. Treaclebunny waved joyfully at Madeline. When they had first arrived at the factory, Mrs. Treaclebunny had started to follow Madeline inside, but Mrs. Bunny had suggested this should be a private moment for Madeline and her parents. Mrs. Treaclebunny had said "Bollocks" and kept hopping, so Mrs. Bunny had had to knock her down and sit on her. She was loath to get up now. Mrs. Treaclebunny made a very comfy seat.

The SWAT team members who had been patrolling around the factory were taking off their cumbersome fake hound heads and wiping the sweat from their foreheads now that it was clear the danger was past.

Tsk, tsk, they will need a furatologist *for sure,* thought Mrs. Bunny.

"I can never thank you enough," said Madeline to the chief of the SWAT team as they all converged.

"All in a day's work, all in a day's work," said the chief. "I think Rabbitville can sleep safely tonight."

"But won't the foxes come back?" asked Madeline.

"Not once they've heard hounds," said the chief. "No, they've abandoned this site for good. They'll start up somewhere else. They always do. But the Treaclebunny factory is safe from them. And I should think you are too. You've got the taint of hounds on you now. That's what we call it. The taint of hounds. Once foxes associate you with a fox hunt, they stay clear of you forever."

Mr. Bunny, who had just pulled up in the Smart car, saw Madeline with what could only be her parents and zipped right over.

"Everyone's safe? Thank goodness. Mrs. Bunny, you should have waited for me, but never mind. And how do you do?" He turned to Flo and Mildred. "You *are* the irresponsible, wretched Flo and Mildred, I presume?"

"Don't be rude," hissed Mrs. Bunny. "He means, uh, happy to meet you."

"I do not," said Mr. Bunny. "For a long time now I've wanted to give the two of you a piece of my mind and . . ."

But Flo and Mildred didn't seem to hear him. Through all the bunnies' talk, they stared blankly. Now Mildred turned to Madeline and said, "Were you talking to that rabbit?"

"Of course I was," said Madeline. "Didn't you hear anything they said?"

"Well, we heard something," said Flo. "But nothing we could understand. Do you understand Rabbit? You know, I think I *did* pick up a certain amount of Fox the last few days. Try this—*Parlez-vous foxeroo?*"

"That's French," said Mr. Bunny coldly, but Flo, of course, didn't understand him.

"Well, perhaps you'd like to translate," said Mr. Bunny to Madeline. "You can tell your father that of all the irresponsible, careless excuses for a father—"

"No need, Mr. Bunny," said Madeline hastily. "I'm fine.

And I figure if they can survive by caring for themselves so well, then maybe I don't have to change so many lightbulbs for them either. Maybe from now on they can change a few of their own. It actually makes me feel kind of . . . free. Does that make sense?"

"Not to me," said Mr. Bunny, giving Flo a swift kick in the shin.

"Ow," said Flo. "That's a mean bunny."

"You ain't seen nothing yet!" yelled Mr. Bunny, preparing to launch another frontal assault, but Mrs. Bunny restrained him and turned to Madeline.

"It makes perfect sense," she said. "I think you're quite wise. Now, I don't know about you, but I could use a nice soothing cup of tea."

"Me too," said Madeline.

"Well, never mind, some people will no doubt get what's coming to them someday," said Mr. Bunny, squaring his shoulders with dignity. He turned to Mrs. Bunny and said sotto voce, "You realize, if you weren't here I would have pulverized that ridiculous hippie."

"I know, dear," said Mrs. Bunny. "You're quite fierce. But I don't think it's what Madeline wants. Let's go get a cake out of the freezer."

"Ooo," said Mr. Bunny. "Cake!"

But perhaps Mr. Bunny would have been gratified had he heard what the foxes were saying at that moment. While the bunnies and Flo and Mildred were sorting themselves out, the foxes were speeding in their car past the edge of the Cowichan Valley and up a mountain until they found a house, empty, with a FOR SALE sign on it and full of furniture that had been inexplicably Krazy Glued to the floor. They decided to settle there for the time being. Frederick Fox unloaded the Tupperwares of finger food from the trunk.

"Do you think they bought that it was eggplant paste in the finger sandwiches?" asked Ferdinand. "Are hoomans that stupid? Didn't they know?"

"Of course they knew," said the Grand Poobah. He paused a second and smiled. "But . . . they were hungry."

* * *

"Oh my goodness, the thought of cake almost made me forget. We have no time for tea! We have no time for cake!" said Mr. Bunny as they made their way toward the Smart car. "We have the graduation ceremony to make!"

"MY GRADUATION!" cried Madeline. "I completely forgot! But can we get there in time?"

"What we?" said Flo. "And why are you asking me? I don't know what time it starts."

"I wasn't, I was talking to the Bunnys," said Madeline.

"Oh yeah, the bunnies 'talk,'" said Flo, making quote marks with his fingers.

"What, now you don't believe the Bunnys talk?" said Madeline in dismay. "But just a second ago you were talking about learning Fox."

"Hey, yeah. But, like, suppose we were drugged by our kidnappers so we just *thought* they were foxes?"

"How are we going to get to Uncle Runyon's?" asked Mildred. "Flo, if we're drugged or dreaming, maybe we can just levitate there." They closed their eyes and tried it.

"That is completely ridiculous," said Mr. Bunny.

"I know," said Madeline, sighing. "But I guess grown-ups can never totally believe in talking animals."

"Who are you talking to?" asked Mildred.

"Listen," said Madeline. "I know you think you're dreaming, but just go with this plan. The Bunnys can drive you. It will be a squish, but the two of you can pile into Mr. Bunny's Smart car. I'll ride on the back of Mrs. Treaclebunny's scooter."

"Levitating is more eco-friendly, but whatever," said Flo, shrugging.

"But we've got to hurry," said Madeline. "Mrs. Bunny needs to be in Comox in time for Prince Charles's parade."

"Oh man, you'd think that since this is, like, a dream, you'd give that whole prince thing a rest," said Flo. "Like he's so special, you gotta go see him even in dreams."

Mrs. Bunny's fur ruffled. "He certainly *is* special! Prince Charles didn't ask for his job. He was born into it. But still he does it. He spends his whole life going to boring old ceremonies and teas and honorings not because he thinks *he's* special but because others have put that value on him and by showing up he makes *them* feel so. You might think about that," she added pointedly.

But, of course, Flo and Mildred couldn't hear her. All they heard were some vaguely rabbity sounds. This frustrated Mrs. Bunny. So she kicked them.

"OW!" said Flo.

"OW!" said Mildred.

"Mrs. *Bunny*!" said Mr. Bunny in amazement. "I've never seen this side of you, but I rather like it."

"Oh dear," said Mrs. Bunny, looking alarmed. "You'd better get them away from me. I've never done anything like that before and I don't want to do it again. You drive them to Uncle Runyon's. I'll go on the scooter with Madeline and Mrs. Treaclebunny. There's something I have to get before we go up-island anyway. Meet us at the hutch, Mr. Bunny."

"Are you sure you don't want to go to the graduation?" asked Madeline as her father got into the car.

"Not even in my dreams, man," said Flo.

"Maybe I should tell Flo that if Uncle Runyon is awake, he should let him know that I can understand animal languages," whispered Madeline to Mr. Bunny. "Uncle Runyon says scientists have been searching for such a person. I could be crucial to his research."

Mr. Bunny grabbed Madeline roughly by the ankle and dragged her away for a moment.

"Do NOT, for heaven's sake, tell anyone any such thing!"

he whispered fiercely. "Do you know what such scientists will do if they get ahold of you? They'll keep you in a cage and study you. You'll be poked and prodded and given injections of who knows what and then tossed on the scrap heap as soon as they're done with you. I hate to paint such a dreadful picture, but I must impress upon you the need to keep this quiet. I swear to you, Madeline, such things have been done to bunnies."

Madeline turned pale. Not because she believed that she would be put in a cage, but because she suddenly realized all the dreadful things that had happened to rabbits at the hands of her species. They might put *Mr. and Mrs. Bunny* in a cage and study *them*.

"You're right," said Madeline to Mr. Bunny. "I won't tell a soul."

Then Madeline said goodbye to her parents and she and Mrs. Bunny leapt behind Mrs. Treaclebunny and off they scooted for the hutch. Mr. Bunny put on his disco driving shoes, ignoring Flo's comments about cool retro footwear, and drove as swiftly as he could to the manor house.

When Flo and Mildred got to Uncle Runyon's, they found

him sitting in the garden. He had just recently come out of his coma. They gave him an abbreviated version of what had happened. Flo kept insisting he was dreaming, and Uncle Runyon said a lot could be blamed on a high fever. Nobody wanted to voice the opinion that it had all been real.

"What was the coma like, man?" asked Flo. "Were there any, oh, say, rabbits in hound costumes?"

"Noooo, can't say there were. Not that I noticed, anyway," drawled Uncle Runyon, clearing his throat. "Actually, it was very refreshing. But no time for any more comas. I have quit my job as a decoder. Too dangerous. Gets people kidnapped. Want a more peaceful life. Besides, I have important work to do. I'm going to Africa to study elephant language."

"Wow," said Flo. "That's, like, so synchronistic. I almost learned Fox."

"You don't say," said Uncle Runyon, and rolled his eyes.

"Yeah, and there's this rabbit that was talking to Madeline."

Flo looked around for Mr. Bunny to corroborate, but he had already hopped back to his car and was out of sight behind the bushes. "In my drugged dream, of course," he added hastily.

"Where is Madeline?" asked Uncle Runyon.

"She went to her graduation," said Mildred. "It's as well.

Flo and I are still not quite right. We were definitely kidnapped and drugged."

"Yes, yes, let's not replay those old tapes," said Uncle Runyon. "As long as Madeline is fine. That's the important thing. How it happened will always be a little hazy. I'll have Jeeves take you to the ferry now. Say goodbye to Madeline for me. I leave tomorrow. Thank goodness Jeeves goes with me. He's an excellent butler."

Curses, thought Mr. Bunny, who couldn't help overhearing this last part. If Mrs. Bunny heard this, she would think she was right about Jeeves. What she didn't understand was that when good butlers went bad they were the worst. This Jeeves fellow would bear watching.

Then he got into his car and drove like the wind to collect her and Madeline.

Mrs. Bunny and Madeline were in the driveway, talking to Mrs. Treaclebunny.

"You see, Mrs. Bunny," said Mr. Bunny, after letting Madeline know that her uncle was out of his coma and would be going to Africa soon with Jeeves. "The butler appears innocent, but he was at the center of things with all that burning. Just as I thought."

"What in the world are you talking about?" asked Mrs. Bunny, who really wished Mr. Bunny would let the butler thing drop once and for all. Especially as it was so apparent he had been wrong from the beginning.

"The burning was a *smokescreen*! That's where the term comes from. I knew I would have to explain this to you." Mr. Bunny was quite pleased with this spontaneous stroke of genius.

"Whatever you say," said Mrs. Bunny. She was getting very tired of detecting. Perhaps it was time to buy new hats.

Just then there was a great commotion. A cloud of dust came down the road. When it got closer they saw who it was.

"THE MARMOT!" cried Madeline in surprise.

"Oh my, oh my, oh my," The Marmot said over and over as he ran up to them. "It came to me this morning. In a dream! I remembered the rest of the file card. It was a recipe. Take two pulverized rabbits, stir with a rubber—there's the word *rubber* I remembered—spatula into five egg yolks with some grated chocolate. Bake in a three-hundred-fifty-degree oven until done for rabbit soufflé. WELL? Aren't I a clever marmot? You rabbits think you're so smart, but, you see, a marmot always saves the day!"

The Bunnys stood agog, not knowing what to say, until Mrs. Treaclebunny decided to take The Marmot home with her to give him some tea. She was banking on using him afterward to wash her windows. Wrung out properly, a marmot made an excellent squeegee. "Come along, Marmot."

"Call me The."

"I'll do nothing of the sort. Hurry up, I've made some very nice blueberry tarts. And what kind of a soufflé doesn't use egg whites?" she said. "It's just as I suspected, foxes can't cook."

"I want garlic bread," he could be heard saying as they headed to her house.

"You're getting blueberry tarts," said Mrs. Treaclebunny. "Or you're getting nothing at all."

"But I saved the day," protested The Marmot.

"*I* saved the day, everyone agrees on that. I was the one who told Mrs. Bunny about the factory. I led the rescue operation with my intrepid driving."

"I want garlic bread."

"Blueberry tarts for you. I tried making a prune plum tart, but it exploded. Odd. I am thinking of writing a cookbook about it. *Recipes for Disaster,* I will call it," said Mrs. Treaclebunny. "Say, want a few bolts of rubber? It makes swell wallpaper."

"And so," said Madeline to Mr. Bunny as they drove up to Comox. "The rubber clue wasn't about the rubber factory, the exploding industrial rubber or even the rubber lining for the bonnets."

"There was all too much rubber in this case," said Mrs. Bunny. "It just got confusing."

"So my parents are fine," Madeline said, sighing contentedly. "Jeeves and Uncle Runyon are going to Africa, the foxes are gone. All's well that ends well, and I guess I can parade with you, Mrs. Bunny, since I can't go to graduation. Not without white shoes."

Mrs. Bunny handed her the package she had come back to the hutch to collect.

Madeline opened it. "White shoes! Oh, Mrs. Bunny, they're beautiful. Did you knit them?"

"Out of used dental floss!" interjected Mr. Bunny.

"How . . . nice," said Madeline.

"If you like, I can make you a sweater to match," said Mrs.

Bunny happily. "But it will take longer because I have to use up an awful lot of floss first."

"That's wonderful. But don't feel you need to hurry. I know how busy you are . . . ," said Madeline.

"Look!" shouted Mrs. Bunny as they approached Comox. "They're gathering!"

And sure enough, buses were stopping and bunnies were hopping out, wearing the most amazing assortment of avant-garde bonnets.

"What happened to the bonnets?" asked Mrs. Bunny. "They're either terribly high-fashion or they're old bonnets that have been ripped to shreds and glued back together hastily in buses while driving up-island."

"Odd," said Mr. Bunny. "Say, Mrs. Bunny, how much do you like that hat club, anyway?"

"Oh!" shouted Madeline. "Look over there! It's Prince Charles! It's the cavalcade! Look at all those limousines gathering! Quick, Mrs. Bunny, you must get in line! The parade is starting!"

"Don't be silly, dear, there are always parades, but there's only one grade five graduation for you. Come on, Mr. Bunny, let's hurry to the school. We want to get good seats."

Soon the Bunnys were seated in the back of the auditorium by the door. They didn't have a very good view, but they felt they'd better be near an exit in case some humans got all exercised about rabbits being in the building. They didn't want to cause a scene on Madeline's big day.

Madeline sat up on stage with the other fifth graders, wearing her white tissue gown and her dental floss shoes.

"She looks so beautiful!" sighed Mrs. Bunny.

"Yes, she's a cutie. Say, I painted her name on the cottage before I left this morning and she hasn't noticed it yet. Right over the door. It says 'Madeline' in blue letters," said Mr. Bunny. "I thought it would be a nice surprise for her tonight when she comes home."

Mrs. Bunny screwed her nose up. "Oh, Mr. Bunny," she said, and a big tear started to drip down her face. "You know after graduation we have to drive Madeline to the ferry, don't you? That that's where we're going after this?"

"Oh!" said Mr. Bunny, and he hopped around in a circle in agitation. "Oh!"

"Stop hopping, someone will notice!" hissed Mrs. Bunny.

"Oh," he said a bit more quietly, and bit his lip. "I knew that. I meant, she'd see it when she came to visit."

"I know that's what you meant," said Mrs. Bunny.

"Unless she says she wants to live with us and not with those useless parents of hers. Then she can. That would be okay, wouldn't it?"

"Of course it would," said Mrs. Bunny, and squeezed his arm, but then their attention was diverted. The prince had arrived and everyone was standing to sing "God Save the Queen" and "O, Canada." After that there were speeches and finally the awards. As each child was called for her award, she came to the center of the stage, where Prince Charles bent forward, handed it to her and said "Congratulations." Finally Madeline's name was called.

"What's he saying? Look!" said Mr. Bunny. "He's talking longer to her than to anyone else."

What Prince Charles said to Madeline was "What smashing shoes! What are they made of?"

"Thank you, used dental floss," said Madeline, turning scarlet.

"Brilliant, absolutely brilliant!" said Prince Charles. "Did you make them?"

"No," said Madeline. "It was a . . . a friend." But how could she not give Mrs. Bunny credit, after all she had done? "It

was a rabbit, actually. Mrs. Bunny. I spent some time with her and Mr. Bunny. I can hear them speak. I understand their language."

"Ah," said Prince Charles. "I've often heard animals speak. Plants too. It's all a matter of noticing, isn't it? The richness of our lives depends on what we are willing to notice and what we are willing to believe. Of course, I get crucified in the press for talking to my plants, but it's awfully rude not to talk back to anyone who speaks to you, isn't it?"

Madeline just nodded.

"Well, congratulations," said Prince Charles, and then it was someone else's turn.

Madeline went back to her chair, her heart racing and her face still brilliant red. The girl next to her had won the math award. Her name was Katherine and she was in Madeline's class, but Madeline knew her only slightly. Katherine leaned over to Madeline and whispered, "What was he *saying* to you? You were up there forever."

"He liked my shoes," said Madeline.

"Yeah, they're cool," said Katherine. "They look like they're made out of dental floss."

"They are," said Madeline.

"I hope it wasn't used," said Katherine, and then they giggled at how ridiculous *that* would be. There was a pause and then Katherine whispered, "Hey, do you want to sleep over at my house sometime?"

"Yes," said Madeline, "that would be great."

They beamed at each other and then went back to watching the next award.

When the ceremony ended, Madeline raced off to tell Mrs. Bunny what Prince Charles had said about her shoes. Mrs. Bunny glowed as they tripped off happily to the parking lot. Nobody seemed to notice that Madeline was going off to a car with a couple of rabbits, which just went to show that Prince Charles was right. It was all a matter of noticing.

"Oh, and I made a friend! Her name is Katherine. We're going to have a *sleepover*! First at her house and then, maybe, on Hornby!"

"Ah!" said Mr. Bunny. "It's off to the ferries, then."

It was a quiet ride. Mrs. Bunny could not bear to look at Mr. Bunny's face the whole way. They pulled up just in time to hear the ferry tooting its warning signal, and so there was only a quick hug before Madeline raced off to get her ticket.

"Thank you! Thank you for everything! I'll come back and visit as soon as I can," she called over her shoulder, and ran to the ticket booth as the ferry tooted again, so that she never heard Mr. Bunny call, "Madeline, don't go! Come back! Come live with us!"

When the ferry pulled away, Madeline ran to the rail and looked for the Bunnys, but she couldn't see them over the crush of big people and cars at the dock, and then the ferry turned and pointed itself in the direction of Denman Island. By the time Madeline caught the ferry from Denman to Hornby, the sun had set and the last ride was under a starry sky.

At first she watched the waves rolling in the moonlight and then, closer into the bay, the ocean suddenly lit up as if a flashlight were shining beneath it. And then again in another place. And then the crest of a wave was alight for a moment.

Phosphorescence, thought Madeline excitedly. She had learned about it at school but never seen it. Small plankton called dinoflagellates must have made their way into the bay. Her teacher had said they flashed when the water was disturbed or crustaceans were trying to eat them. Scientists thought they flashed to warn other plankton or to distract the crustaceans. But Madeline liked that no one really knew why they did it. What had Uncle said? That Einstein believed that an underlying reality existed in nature that was independent of our ability to observe or measure it. An underlying reality. And bunnies, thought Madeline. She watched a long time as light appeared miraculously from underneath this and then that corner of the dark sea. And then the ferry docked and she followed the moonlight home.

Mr. Bunny was grumpy for many days afterward. Then one morning Mrs. Bunny brought him a scone and some tea outside and placed a thick manila envelope in front of him.

"What's this?" he asked.

"I have decided I am tired of being detectives," said Mrs. Bunny.

"Oh dear," said Mr. Bunny. "I see something expensive on the horizon."

"*Au contraire*," said Mrs. Bunny with dignity. "This time I am going to *make* us some money. I have written up the whole story of our detecting adventures. I am going to be a writer. And so are you."

"I don't think you can just decide to be a writer," said Mr. Bunny.

"Yes you can. In fact, I have done it. Now I want you to drive me into town for my hat club meeting and while I'm there, mail this manuscript to Bunny Publishing."

Mr. Bunny sighed. "Do you really think you should go to another meeting after the, uh, incident?" (As they referred to Mr. Bunny's hat-tearing caprice.)

"Oh, don't be silly. The ladies all think the male of the species is more or less insane. They have, if anything, *more* sympathy for me than ever."

"Harumph," said Mr. Bunny, sliding the manuscript out of the envelope and starting to read it. *"Madeline and the Detectives, by Mrs. Bunny,"* he read.

"Catchy title, huh?" said Mrs. Bunny.

"But we were the heroes! We saved the day and it doesn't even mention us by name!"

"Not important, it's a wonderful title."

"It's a pooey title. What you want to call it is *Mr. and Mrs. Bunny—Detectives Extraordinaire!*"

"I do not," said Mrs. Bunny as they got into the Smart car and started for town. "I want to call it *Madeline and the Detectives.*"

"*Mr. and Mrs. Bunny—Detectives Extraordinaire!* What a bestseller ring that has about it!"

"*Madeline and the Detectives,*" said Mrs. Bunny, crossing her arms. "And might I say what a tin ear you have, Mr. Bunny."

Back and forth they went all the way to the hat shoppe. When Mrs. Bunny got out, she put the manuscript back in the envelope and carefully sealed it. "There," she said, "the deed is done. I'll see you at four."

"As you like," said Mr. Bunny with dignity, and drove to the post office. He got in line and was just about to hand the envelope to the postmistress for weighing when he spied some manila envelopes for sale. He bought one and addressed it. He opened the envelope Mrs. Bunny had sealed and took out the manuscript. He looked at the first page, did a little scribbling and then put it in the new envelope for the postmistress to mail.

"In time Mrs. Bunny will see I am right," he said to himself. Then he hopped happily back into the warm summer air.

Everyone's favorite bunnies are back!

Turn the page for a sneak peek at the newest adventures of Madeline and the Bunnys in

⊨SHIPBOARD BUNNIES⊨

"I t was very nice of the hat club to send a fruit basket to our stateroom," said Mrs. Bunny with a note of false cheer. She was putting on her long sparkly formal gown for their first shipboard dinner.

"Nothing about this cruise bears any resemblance to the brochures," grumbled Mr. Bunny, struggling into his tuxedo shirt. His furry tummy kept bursting through between the buttons. That was what it was to be a rabbit. Endless tucking in of loose fur. "Those big staterooms in the pictures?" Mr. Bunny looked around the tiny room he and Mrs. Bunny were sharing. There were two tiny twin beds and practically nowhere for their luggage. "Not."

"Oh dear," said Mrs. Bunny as she tried on her earrings. It was difficult to wear dangling earrings when your ears were so long. Her earrings kept dangling down into her ear canals. "Too much?" She was hoping to distract Mr. Bunny from his mood of doom and gloom. So far nothing about this trip was as she had promised. It wasn't "Better than home!" "Full of luxury and expensive free bath products for Mrs. Bunny!" "Endless service at no extra cost!" "Huge stateroom with quality linens!" So far it was just a small room in the sub-sub-basement level of the ship. That they would not be riding up on top, she already knew. The bunny cruises did at least tell you the animal deck was below the human one. Unfortunately, although the brochures stated this plainly, the pictures they provided were for the human quarters. It was very trying to be a vacationing rabbit.

"Well, there had better just be a gym. Mr. Bunny needs his hopping," said Mr. Bunny.

Mrs. Bunny sighed again.

At that moment there was a knock on the door. Mr. Bunny was trying to get his bow tie to lie evenly over a particularly cumbersome tuft of fur, so Mrs. Bunny answered it.

It was Mrs. Treaclebunny. "Do you have any Flit?" she asked. "I forgot to pack mine. Always take it when traveling to spray the beds. You never know. Bugs. For all we know, Bug Cruises are putting their travelers up in our rooms. Saves a lot of money for them."

"I'm sure there are no bugs on this ship," said Mrs. Bunny.

"Well, perhaps not in *my* room," said Mrs. Treaclebunny, looking critically around Mr. and Mrs. Bunny's cramped quarters. She settled herself on Mrs. Bunny's bed. "You must have gone for the economy package."

"We did," said Mr. Bunny. "I'm not shelling out twice the fare for a slightly bigger room."

"Slightly? You could fit ten of your rooms in my room. . . ." Mrs. Treaclebunny's voice trailed off as she looked around. "And where's your champagne and chompies?"

"Chompies?" asked Mrs. Bunny.

"You know, little bite-sized edibles. They always bring them to you before dinner and before bed. That's what Mr. Treaclebunny and I called them. So many and so varied and so rich. We could never finish them although we chomped for all we were worth."

"We, uh, didn't get any chompies," said Mrs. Bunny, looking close to tears.

"Not included in the economy package," said Mr. Bunny. "Who needs them. Look what Mr. Bunny brought!" He went over to his suitcase and triumphantly pulled out a large jar of Cheez Whiz and a box of saltines. "We can make our own chompies!" He proceeded to spread Cheez Whiz on a cracker, getting Cheez Whiz and cracker crumbs everywhere in the attempt. "There," he said when he had managed a few that didn't simply disintegrate all over the floor. He removed some soap packets from a little plastic tray in the bathroom, put his homemade chompies on it and served them forth. "Anyone for a chompie?"

Mrs. Bunny and Mrs. Treaclebunny quickly declined. Mrs. Bunny looked closer to tears than ever.

"Anyhow," said Mrs. Treaclebunny, getting up and spinning around, "what do you think of the dress?"

Both Mrs. Bunny and Mrs. Treaclebunny had been frequenting Bunnydale's with some regularity for the last couple of days. It was one reason the Bunnys were going economy class.

"It's ravishing," said Mrs. Bunny truthfully. Mrs. Treaclebunny was a vision in red sequins. Mrs. Bunny was starting slow with her black chiffon. She wanted to see how sparkly the other bunnies dressed before pulling out the big guns.

"Are you sitting first or second dinner service?" asked Mrs. Treaclebunny. "Second service is the smart one."

"We're sitting first service," said Mr. Bunny. "It's part of our economy package. I much prefer it myself. I do not like having to wait much past five o'clock for my dinner."

"Well, looks like I won't be seeing much of you, then," said Mrs. Treaclebunny, getting up and laughing. "I'm at second service myself. Toodle-oo." And she waltzed out the door.

"Come on, Mrs. Bunny," said Mr. Bunny, jovially taking her elbow and leading her out of their stateroom. "Don't want to be last at the trough."

MRS. BUNNY lives in Rabbitville, in the Cowichan Valley, on Vancouver Island, British Columbia. She is married to Mr. Bunny and has twelve children. This is her first book.

POLLY HORVATH is the author of *My One Hundred Adventures,* an Amazon Best Book of the Year and a NAPPA Gold Award Winner; and *Northward to the Moon,* a Parents' Choice Gold Award Winner. Her other books include *The Canning Season,* a National Book Award winner; and *Everything on a Waffle,* a Newbery Honor Book. *Publishers Weekly* has praised her writing as "unruly, unpredictable, and utterly compelling," and *Booklist* has called it "as foamy as waves, as gritty as sand, or as deep as the sea." This is her first translation. Polly Horvath lives in Metchosin, British Columbia. Learn more at pollyhorvath.com.

SOPHIE BLACKALL received the Ezra Jack Keats New Illustrator Award. She is the illustrator of *Edwin Speaks Up* by April Stevens, called "stylish" and "a read-aloud favorite" by *Publishers Weekly; Big Red Lollipop* by Rukhsana Khan, a *New York Times* Best Illustrated Book; *Meet Wild Boars* by Meg Rosoff, a *Bulletin* Blue Ribbon Book; the Ivy and Bean series by Annie Barrows; and other children's books. A native of Australia, Sophie now lives in Brooklyn, New York. Visit her at sophieblackall.com.